TERROR AT NORTHWOOD!

"It's a G-r-r-rat attack!" a wide-eyed Peter growled in a low voice. He swallowed. "A real one!"

"That's Cornelius Grat?" Shane asked, incredulous at finally laying eyes on Northwood's legendary next-door neighbor.

The wild-eyed man leered, showing a row of broken, yellow teeth. "I'm warning you now, if I catch any of you on my land again, I'll . . . I'll chop you up for firewood!"

Finally it was too much. Everyone started laughing, unable to hold back any longer.

Cornelius Grat's face turned red with embarrassment—and anger. His eyes seemed to turn darker, as if storm clouds roiled behind the irises. He raised his arm, and pointed a crooked finger. "I'll get you!" he hollered, "I'll get all of you!"

This book is a presentation of Newfield Publications, Inc.
Newfield Publications offers book clubs for children from
preschool through high school. For further information
write to: **Newfield Publications, Inc.,** 4343 Equity Drive,
Columbus, Ohio 43228.

Published by arrangement with Puffin Books,
a division of Penguin Books USA Inc.
Newfield Publications is a federally registered
trademark of Newfield Publications, Inc.

PUFFIN BOOKS
Published by the Penguin Group
Penguin Books USA Inc., 375 Hudson Street, New York, New York 10014, U.S.A.
Penguin Books Ltd, 27 Wrights Lane , London W8 5TZ, England
Penguin Books Australia Ltd, Ringwood, Victoria, Australia
Penguin Books Canada Ltd, 10 Alcorn Avenue, Toronto, Onartio, Canada M4V 3B2
Penguin Books (N.Z.) Ltd, 182-190 Wairau Road, Auckland 10, New Zealand

Penguin Books Ltd, Registered Offices: Harmondsworth, Middlesex, England

First published in the United States of America by Puffin Books,
a division of Penguin Books USA Inc., 1993

Pearce, J.C.
Tug of war / by J.C. Pearce.
p.   cm.—(Foul play; 5)
Summary: A madman stalks the participants of a winter intermural competition at a
boarding school in the Adirondack Mountains.
ISBN 0-14-036663-6.
[1. Horror stories.   2. Adirondack Mountains (N.Y.)—Fiction.
3. Schools—Fiction.]   I. Title.   II. Series.
PZ7.P3148Tu 1993
[Fic]—dc20   93-15037   CIP   AC

Printed in the United States of America

High Flyer™ is a trademark of Puffin Books, a division of Penguin Books USA Inc.

FOUL PLAY

TUG-OF-WAR

BY J.C. PEARCE

PUFFIN BOOKS

CHAPTER 1

"Gimme that!" Mark Lepine shouted, grabbing the soup ladle in Shane Bradford's hand. Shane had just dipped it into the huge, stainless steel tureen on the dining hall counter when Mark suddenly appeared from the kitchen. Mark was the class president—and a star athlete at Northwood, a boarding school in upstate New York.

"Hey, I'm new here," Shane protested. "I thought it was self-serve." After a short tug-of-war with Mark, he let go of the ladle, but it was too late. Tomato soup spilled all over the counter.

Lepine leveled his icy blue gaze at Shane. "What a spaz! And you think *you're* going to win the Winter Murals for Apple House? You haven't got a chance, Bradford!"

"If you hadn't pulled the spoon out of his hand, you wouldn't have made the mess, Mark." A girl's voice spoke behind Shane. He turned and saw Lynn Wesley carrying a big metal tray filled with water jugs. Lynn was

1

in Apple House, too, where Shane had lived since he started at Northwood three weeks earlier.

The school was actually part of an old pioneer farm deep in the Adirondack Mountains. And so far north that, as Shane liked to joke, "You could spit and it would land in Canada." Only about a hundred kids were enrolled in Northwood, in the sixth, seventh, and eighth grades. Shane had started his first semester in the eighth grade just after Christmas. His father was a civil engineer, and had accepted a major position in Saudi Arabia building a huge new petrochemical complex. Shane had transferred from his old public school in Philadelphia while his parents moved to Riyadh for a year.

Actually, Northwood seemed more like a village to Shane. Near the old farmhouse, a rustic lodge had been built to house the dining hall, and behind it, classrooms. All the kids lived in modern houses set among the surrounding woods. Every house had a name—like Apple House, Raccoon House, Mountain House, Crow House. Eight kids lived in each. The teachers doubled as house counselors and lived in the houses, too. Mr. Durrell, the history teacher, was in charge of Apple House, along with his wife.

A lot of what the kids learned wasn't in class. Northwood prided itself on teaching hard work and self-reliance. All the students had to do chores around the farm, or help out in the dining hall for part of their credits. Last year the senior classes had even helped build the big new barn.

Mark Lepine was in Crow House and, like Lynn, helped

to serve food in the kitchen for one meal each day. He was the most popular kid at Northwood, but as a new kid Shane had found him kind of bossy. Today was no exception.

"You know you're not supposed to get food unless one of the servers is here," Mark reminded Shane pointedly, ignoring Lynn's comment.

"No one was here," Shane pointed out. "And our table didn't get any soup yet."

"Rules are—" Mark began.

"Get real," Lynn interrupted. "The Quince wants us to use initiative—remember he lectured us all about it last week." Lynn set down her tray, took the ladle from Mark and filled a big enamel bowl full of the creamy red soup. She handed it to Shane to take back to Apple House's table. Then she looked defiantly at Mark. "And Apple House *is* going to win the Winter Murals tomorrow. With Shane on our team this year—"

"You've got half a chance," Mark agreed, nodding at Shane.

Northwood School's annual Winter Murals—a day of ski and toboggan races, ending with a Tug-of-War between the top-scoring houses—were held every year at the end of the January. Mark Lepine had led Crow House to victory for two years in a row, and he was determined to make it three.

"Don't underestimate the competition, Mark," Shane said. "Lynn is the school's cross-country ski champ and I plan to whip you in the downhill. There's no way Crow House can win a third year in a row."

"You know, for a new kid who just started here a few weeks ago, you got a lot of attitude," Mark said.

"It's not attitude," Lynn informed him, anxious to help out her housemate. "It's reality. Shane won the junior league slalom championship for the entire northeast last year."

For a second, Mark just stared at Shane with his mouth open. Shane shrugged and looked embarrassed.

"See you on the hill tomorrow," Lynn said with a final smug glance at Mark. The athletic blonde girl picked up her tray and headed back to the tables.

"She's kidding," Mark stated flatly.

Shane shook his head. "My parents took me skiing practically before I was old enough to walk," he told Mark. "Anyway, I hear you're a real good downhill skier, too. It'll be a great race!"

Mark didn't look as if he agreed. He glanced quickly from side to side to make sure no one was listening. Then, in a low voice, he muttered, "Let me give you some advice, new kid. Don't get in the way of me winning for the third year in a row—or I'll squash you like a bug."

"Chill, Mark," Shane retorted. "I like sports as much as you, but it's just sports—not exactly hand-to-hand combat in total war."

But Mark wasn't listening. He stormed back into the kitchen to finish his chores. Shane rolled his eyes, and began walking down the long rows of tables with the bowl of hot soup.

On the way, he passed a huge old oil painting of a gray-haired man wearing a blue and white Continental

Army uniform from the War of Independence. On his first day at Northwood, Shane had learned it was a portrait of Benjamin Quincy, the ancestor of Northwood's headmaster, Thelonius Quincy, who had turned the old farm into Northwood School. Even if he was a Revolutionary War hero, Shane thought he looked cold and mean, with a pinched mouth, glowering eyes, and huge bushy sideburns that grew right down his face to his cleft chin.

For more than two hundred years, the Quincy family had owned almost all the land in a narrow valley surrounded by three rugged Adirondack mountains. In the east, Morning Peak was squat and rounded, like a great hump covered with forest. A long toboggan run had been built in the snow on its gentle lower slopes. On the north side was Mount Lookout, which was also covered with trees. However, several downhill ski runs had been cleared through the woods and there was a T-bar ride that took skiers to the top.

But the tallest mountain was in the west. Mount Fear rose over the valley, its jagged, rocky peak like a giant broken tooth. A few days after he arrived at Northwood, Shane learned that Mount Fear had a legend. It was supposed to be haunted by its own ghost!

During the Revolutionary War, Benjamin Quincy and his neighbor, Martin Grat, discovered that the British were launching a surprise attack against the town of Peace Lake, just on the other side of Mount Fear. Since the road out of the narrow valley was guarded by enemy soldiers, the two men climbed Mount Fear in a snowstorm to warn the town. They had to cross a narrow and dangerous ledge. In the icy weather, Martin Grat slipped and fell to his death. Benjamin Quincy got through to warn the town and as a result, the British had been defeated. But local legend had it that the ghost of Martin Grat still haunted Mount Fear.

Shane didn't believe in ghosts, but Mount Fear still gave him the creeps. Maybe it was only because it was winter, he thought. All the trees were bare, and the valley was covered with snow. But from the first moment he set eyes on Mount Fear, Shane felt as if the mountain were somehow alive, brooding silently over some terrible, ancient horror beyond anything he could imagine.

Shane reached the table nearest the front door, where the other kids from Apple House—Peter, Darlene, Jeff, Corky, and Delia—were waiting, and put the big bowl of tomato soup on the table. All the kids in Crow House—Serge, Priscilla, Keith, Sloan, Sue, and Renaldo—sat at the next table over. Crow was the most athletic of all the houses, and Mark Lepine's sidekick, Serge Williams, was taunting Peter about the Winter Murals. Shane figured Serge carried a chip on his shoulder because he was short for his age.

"Hey, Peter, I hear you're captain of your house's toboggan team," Serge called over from the next table. "That'll be a laugh. You're so fat the toboggan won't go anywhere."

All the kids in Crow House laughed.

"Yeah? Well I got news, Serge," Peter shot back. "It's a downhill race and my extra weight will make us go even faster." It was true Peter was on the heavy side, but jokes about his weight never seemed to bother him.

"No way, Peter," Serge taunted. "And even if you do, Crow House'll win all the other contests—*and* the Quincy Cup for the third . . . year . . . in . . . a . . . row!" he emphasized.

"Dream along with meeeeee!" Peter started singing loudly.

Serge stopped smiling and looked annoyed. "And as Team Leader, Mark Lepine's name will be up on North-wood's Honor Roll again."

"And he'll be the first student in Northwood's history to do it three years in a row," Priscilla added.

"Bet you he won't," Peter sing-songed.

"No way," Serge interjected, turning to Priscilla. "He already owes me two Snickers bars from last week," he explained. "We bet on the Rose Bowl game and my team won."

Serge turned to Peter. "Hey, Dark, when do I get my Snickers bars? Or do I have to pound you for them?"

"You touch me and I'll sic old man Grat on you for a Grat attack!" Peter snapped back. Cornelius Grat was Northwood's weird next-door neighbor, and the descendent of Martin Grat, who had fallen off Mount Fear two hundred years earlier. Shane had never set eyes on him, but he'd heard Grat was totally bonkers. There were even rumors that every ten years or so, a Northwood student disappeared, supposedly into torture chambers deep in the ground beneath Grat's tumbledown, decaying farm-house. Peter had made up the phrase "Grat attack" only a few weeks earlier, but it had quickly spread through the school as a wisecrack.

Just then, Northwood's headmaster, Thelonius Quincy, walked to the front of the room and tapped at the lectern. His long bushy sideburns grew straight out from his cheeks and almost down to his cleft chin, giving him a mane like a lion's, as well as a striking similarity to his ancestor. But there the resemblance ended. While Benjamin Quincy, the pioneering ancestor, looked stern and forbidding, Mr. Quincy was usually smiling and pleasant. He was a wildly popular teacher and ran Northwood with a steady hand. Behind his back, all the kids knew him affectionately as "The Quince."

Quincy looked out over the dining hall waiting for the students to stop talking. He made announcements after every meal.

"About the Winter Murals tomorrow, I have some good news," the Quince began. "According to the weather forecast, an inch of snow will fall overnight—perfect powder for the ski runs. Tomorrow is expected to be sunny and almost warm."

Around the dining hall, different kids starting cheering. The Quince put up his hands to stop them. "Every house has been asked to select the best competitors for the Murals. I'd like last year's winner—the winner of the last two years, actually, and our class president as well—to come out."

Mark Lepine appeared from the kitchen, still wearing a long white apron, and wiping his hands on a towel. A bunch of girls at a table up near the front jumped up, as if on cue, and started shouting Mark's name. Mark blushed and waved at them.

"Once again the Quincy Cup is up for grabs," Mark began, gesturing to the huge glistening silver trophy being hoisted aloft by his housemates. "Except I intend to grab it again this year!"

This time, the entire school broke out in a mixture of cheers and good-natured boos. A smile spread across Mark's face. "Now let's go around the dining hall so every house can introduce their competitors." Mark flashed another smile. "That way I can get a preview of my competition."

One by one, the name of each house was called, and the team members stood up. When it was Apple House's turn, Shane, Lynn, and Peter stood. Crow House was Mark, Serge, and Priscilla. When that was over, Mark gave a short speech about how everyone had to try their hardest. "Remember what Northwood is all about," he concluded. "Teamsmanship and strategy!"

Suddenly, without warning, the double front doors of the dining hall burst open and a blast of icy cold wind entered the room. A big, shambling man with a wild mane of dirty gray hair barged into the dining hall, shaking his fists in the air.

"Thieves!" he yelled at the top of his lungs. "Spies! I'll stop you even if I have to kill you all!"

CHAPTER 2

Every pair of eyes in the dining hall was riveted to the great bearlike old man framed by the dining hall's double doors. He had a bushy black beard, streaked with gray. His eyes were so bloodshot that the rims were red, and there were great dark bags under them, as if he hadn't slept in months. He wore a dirty red plaid jacket, and his long, stringy gray hair stuck out every which way from beneath a bright red hunter's cap.

"It's a G-r-r-rat attack!" a wide-eyed Peter growled in a low voice. He swallowed. "A real one!"

"That's Cornelius Grat?" Shane asked, incredulous at finally laying eyes on Northwood's legendary next-door neighbor.

"I'm warning you for the last time, Quincy," Grat thundered, shaking his fists at the headmaster. "Next time you send your students on to my property to spy I'll—"

"This is preposterous!" the Quince exclaimed, almost

10

stammering with—Shane couldn't tell exactly whether it was anger or surprise. Maybe both. Shane could almost feel the hatred coming in chilling waves from the mountainous figure in the doorway. Shane shivered.

"Don't lie to me!" the man shouted furiously. "I know you're sending your students over to spy on me! Trying to drive me off my land just like the Quincys always have!"

Shane saw the headmaster stiffen and turn white.

"Enough, *Mister* Grat!" Mr. Quincy's voice boomed authoritatively. "I will not have my family name besmirched with this . . . this . . . insane grudge your family has carried on for two centuries! You are not welcome on this property. If you have a complaint, then call the police just as I intend to do right now unless you turn around and instantly leave these premises!"

"Way to go, Quince," Peter whispered quietly, nudging Shane in the ribs.

Cornelius Grat stopped, and for a moment seemed to be ready to retreat.

"Out!" Thelonius Quincy shouted, pointing dramatically toward the open doors. "Out!"

The wild-eyed man took a few steps backward until he was even with the doorframe. He tore his gaze away from the headmaster and looked at the roomful of kids. He leered at them, showing a row of broken, yellow teeth. "I'm warning you now, if I catch any of you on my land again, I'll . . . I'll chop you up for firewood!"

Finally it was too much. Serge let out a Bronx cheer that broke the breathless silence in the dining hall. Everyone started laughing, unable to hold back any longer.

"Serge Williams!" Thelonius Quincy said sternly, angrily eyeing the last table.

Cornelius Grat's face turned red with embarrassment—and anger. From where Shane sat, he could see a thick vein pulsing on the side of the mountain man's forehead. His eyes seemed to turn darker, as if storm clouds roiled behind the irises. He raised his arm, and pointed a crooked finger at the kids in the room. "I'll get you!" he hollered, "I'll get all of you!"

Then he turned and walked outside, his red jacket quickly swallowed up by darkness and falling snow.

Quickly, Shane jumped up from his bench and pulled the big doors shut. The howl of the wind stopped abruptly and the sudden silence in the dining hall was eerie. Then everybody started talking at once.

All the houseparents and teachers gathered at the front of the dining hall around the headmaster, conferring with very serious expressions on their faces. The Quince broke away from them and stood before the students. He cleared his throat.

"Now you all know that there are some people in this world who are disadvantaged. Unfortunately, we share this valley with one of them. Mr. Grat has a very dangerous temper. If any of you provoke him by trespassing on his land, I will take drastic action. Now you're dismissed. Let's all get a good night's sleep for the Winter Murals tomorrow."

The students filed out of the dining hall. A path called Sky Walk led through trees at the foot of Mount Fear to the houses where the students lived. As the kids in Apple

House walked home, Shane and Lynn fell into step together. Darlene and Jeff were ahead of them, and Peter lagged far behind.

"What was that all about, Grat accusing Quincy of stealing his land?" Shane asked.

Lynn sighed. "It's part of the ghost story of Mount Fear. Two hundred years ago, the Grat family and the Quincys each owned half the valley. But after Martin Grat fell off Mount Fear, the Grats were broke. They had to start selling their land."

"To the Quincy family?" Shane guessed.

"Right," Lynn nodded. "That's what Grat meant when he accused the Quincys of taking his land."

Overhearing their conversation, Darlene and Jeff dropped back to walk beside Shane and Lynn. Outlined by light from a cloud-draped moon, Mount Fear loomed above the trees. Lynn pointed to the sheer granite face just below the peak, glistening strangely through the light snowfall.

"The only way over the mountain to Peace Lake is along a really narrow ledge at the bottom of that cliff," Lynn explained to Shane. "That's where Martin Grat allegedly fell when he and Ben Quincy were trying to get across to warn people that the British army was coming."

"And it's where people still see the ghost lights," Darlene added.

"Wait a second," Shane interrupted. "The *what* lights?"

"Sometimes people see strange lights up on Mount Fear," Jeff said. "Glowing lights that move along the

13

bottom of the cliff as if someone's walking across the ledge. It's supposed to be the ghost of Martin Grat.''

"And people say the ghost lights always appear before a major blizzard," Darlene continued. "Because Martin Grat fell off in a terrible snowstorm."

Jeff snickered and looked at Lynn and Darlene. "Except at Halloween, even when it's not even snowing."

Lynn and Darlene started laughing, until Lynn saw the baffled look on Shane's face. "Last Halloween, Peter and Serge Williams and some other kids climbed up Mount Fear with flashlights and long bamboo poles," she explained. "They were going to scare everyone down here by dangling the flashlights from the ledge to make them look like ghost lights."

"Except word got around about what they were doing," Darlene said. "So some other kids secretly went ahead of them. When Peter and Serge got up to the ledge that leads across the mountain, they heard all these howls and shrieks. Then some ghosts—actually the other kids from Northwood who'd gone up—jumped out from behind rocks to scare them."

"You should have seen Peter's face when he got back to Apple House," Jeff laughed. "He ran all the way down the mountain without stopping. And he looked about as white as a ghost."

"That's because I saw a real ghost!" Peter called out, running to catch up to them.

When he reached their side, Shane smiled at him. "You mean you really saw the ghost of Martin Grat, haunting the ledge where he fell," he joked.

"Nope," Peter said firmly, shaking his head. "I saw the ghost of Benjamin Quincy—doomed to wander forever because of the terrible crime he committed."

"Oh, Peter," Lynn scolded. "That's not true."

Now Shane was totally confused. "What do you mean, Benjamin Quincy's crime? I thought he was a hero for saving Peace Lake from a British attack."

"He did," Peter nodded. "But he also pushed Martin Grat off the ledge so he could buy up the Grats' land and own the whole valley. That's the other version of what happened on Mount Fear two hundred years ago. And when he got to Peace Lake, he told everyone that Martin Grat slipped because of the snowstorm."

"No way!" Lynn objected. "Besides, the Quince is too nice a guy to have a great-great-great-grandfather like that. Whose side are you on, anyway?"

"When I went up there on Halloween, I saw Benjamin Quincy's ghost," Peter insisted. "I recognized it from the big painting in the dining hall. That means Grat's version of the story is the right one—Benjamin Quincy is doomed to wander Mount Fear forever because he was a murderer!"

"It wasn't the ghost of Ben Quincy," Jeff said scornfully. "It was some other kids from Northwood who went up there to scare you."

Peter shook his head silently. "Yeah, some other kids came up there to scare us, and they did scare us—totally. Serge and I started running in different directions. That's when I saw the ghost. Him. The guy in the oil painting."

Darlene and Jeff exchanged a look. "Sure you did,

15

Peter," Darlene said. "You saw someone who just *looked* like the ghost of Ben Quincy."

"I know you don't believe me," Peter said stubbornly. "But I know what I saw."

Shane smiled at him. "I just don't believe in ghosts."

They had reached the walk that led up to Apple House. Peter looked back in the direction they had come.

"Uhh, I left my scarf," he said. "I gotta go back for it."

"In the dining hall?" Lynn asked. "Get it at breakfast."

"Are you kidding? Someone else will be wearing it by then." Peter ran back down Sky Walk. When he was out of sight of Apple House, he darted sideways along the bottom of the hill until he came to a gravel service road that Tiny, the maintenance man, had plowed with the blade on the tractor. The story of the lost scarf was a fib. Peter had other business.

Looking around to be certain he was alone, he jumped over the huge mound of snow on the frozen gravel. On his right was the old barn and the new barn.

He crept around the new barn. The hill rose sharply above him, and he could make out the wooden sides of the toboggan shed. The snow was beginning to fall harder. An icy wind, sharp as razors, whipped the flakes into swirls, and they bit into Peter's face. He knelt at the corner of the shed, and pulled some rocks away from the concrete pad the building sat on, revealing a small dark hole in the side of a cinderblock.

He pulled off his mitten and reached his hand into the hole. "There you are, babies," he muttered happily, pulling out a handful of Snickers bars. There were three. Two for him, and one for Serge. At least it would buy the bully off until he could persuade his mother to send some more.

Candy and chocolate bars were one of the few things that the kids at Northwood were not supposed to have, and any that the teachers found were instantly confiscated. As a result, Peter and a lot of other kids had stashes hidden in secret places. And since sweets were in such short supply, it was a great way to barter with other kids for favors.

Peter put two of the chocolate bars in his pocket and stood up. He peeled the wrapper down off the third one and took a bite. The sweet milk chocolate almost brought tears to his eyes. He heaved a sigh of contentedness, took another bite, and walked out from behind the shed.

Directly in front of him, the jagged peak of Mount Fear was silhouetted against the sky, and lit by the silver glow of the crescent moon. High above him, at the base of the peak where the narrow ledge led across the mountain to the town of Peace Lake, a light flickered through the falling snow, like a glowing orb floating along the base of the cliff!

CHAPTER 3

Peter instantly forgot his stash. Shivers rippled up and down his spine, and he could feel his skin breaking out in goosebumps. *The ghost lights,* he thought. Now he could prove to the other kids that he wasn't lying.

He raced helter-skelter down the frozen gravel road toward Apple House and up the steps to the front porch. He rushed into the house, barely stopping to stomp the snow from his boots.

Shane, Lynn, Darlene, and Jeff were in their reading corners in the living room, a comfortable room with polished oak panelling, and big, overstuffed chairs. Shane turned around when he heard the door open. He saw Peter walk in—his face white and his eyes as big as Frisbees.

"There are ghosts lights up on Mount Fear," Peter exclaimed. "Right on the ledge."

"Uh-oh. That means a blizzard's coming," Darlene blurted.

18

"First," Shane began, gesturing to the light snowfall outside the window, "The weather forecast says no more than an inch of two of snow. And second, there's no such thing as ghosts."

"So, see for yourself," Peter challenged. Without waiting for Shane to answer, the plump boy did an about-face and strode to the front door. When the others made no effort to follow, he turned to face them. "Oh, yeah," he taunted. "Afraid of seeing that you're wrong?"

Shane looked at Lynn. "Well?"

Lynn nodded quickly. They both jumped up, grabbed their coats from hooks in the hall, and stepped outside after Peter.

"This way," Peter said, leading them. "You can see it from the road to the new barn."

They rounded the house and the great mass of Mount Fear came into view, like a giant fist rising up behind the curtains of falling snow. Shane put his hand to his eyes to shield them, and squinted to see. He could barely make out the great face of rock, darker than the forested slopes that sprawled below.

There were no lights on Mount Fear. At least, none that Shane could see.

"What lights?" Lynn asked scornfully.

Peter didn't answer. He peered through the snow at the curving flanks of the great mountain, his eyes rising first to the jagged peak, then to the cliff below. "It was there!" he shouted. He started walking quickly up the service road, leaving a trail of footprints in the newly fallen snow. He felt angry and disappointed at the same time,

19

bummed out because now his friends would think he was a liar, and he *knew* he had seen a light up there. "I swear it!" he called back to them.

He stopped twenty feet away from his friends and stared hard at Mount Fear, silently begging for just a single glimpse, a quick flash of light to persuade his friends.

The mountain was completely dark. Shane and Lynn walked up behind Peter and turned to look around. Shane was looking across the bottom of the snow-covered ski slope to the edge of the great pine forest when he saw the movement of someone darting deeper into the woods.

"Someone's over there!" he said quickly in a hushed voice.

"Where?" Lynn asked.

"On the other side of the slopes, I saw someone in a red jacket run into the forest and head uphill."

Peter and Lynn both looked in the direction that Shane indicated.

"What's up there?" Shane asked.

"Just the shed where the toboggans are stored," Lynn told him. There was a moment of silence. They could almost hear the snow, quintillions of flakes every moment touching the frozen ground.

"The toboggans for the races tomorrow?" Shane asked.

Suddenly, all Peter could think of was his event in the Winter Murals being somehow threatened. "Let's stop him!" he said, bursting into a run toward the storage shed.

"Stop who, from what?" Shane muttered, racing after Peter with Lynn.

When they reached the edge of the forest Peter stopped. In the eerie, sudden silence, Shane heard the wind beating through the needled boughs of pines, as ever more snowflakes danced around them. The aluminum shed was thirty feet away. Enormous footprints led through the shallow snow, past the shed and into the forest.

"Wow," Peter exclaimed quietly. "Looks like Bigfoot's been through here."

"Peter, your imagination is too much," Shane said wearily. He'd just about had it with all this supernatural stuff. "For the last time, there are no ghosts, so naturally there are no ghost lights and Bigfoot doesn't exist except in books and movies." He walked to the nearest footprint, knelt, and looked at it carefully. He stood up and walked back to Lynn and Peter.

"Snowshoes," he announced. "If you look at the prints in the snow real close, you can see the crisscross pattern of the hides that lace the frames together."

Peter shivered. "Grat wears snowshoes sometimes."

"And a red jacket," Lynn pointed out.

"A Grat attack," Peter said in a solemn tone.

Shane eyed his friends. "What's he doing on Quincy land?"

"Looking for students to chop up?" Peter suggested. He shuddered, remembering the eccentric's threat in the dining hall.

"I'm not sure this is something we should joke about,"

21

Lynn said seriously. "I think we should tell the Quince, or something," she added.

"Yeah, right," Shane said skeptically. "Well, Mr. Quincy, see, it's like this," he mimicked. "Peter told us that Martin Grat's ghost was seen flashing some lights on Mount Fear so we went out to look. We didn't see the ghost or the lights, but—"

"We saw old man Grat running around on snowshoes," Peter continued.

"We're not even sure it *was* Grat," Shane said stubbornly.

"Shane, you have to admit it probably was Grat even if we didn't actually see him," Lynn put in. "The red jacket, the snowshoes—who else could it be?"

"Whatever," Shane grumbled. "My point is, we're not even supposed to be running around campus in the middle of the night, we're supposed to be home, studying and resting up for the Winter Murals, which are tomorrow. Aside from that, we really don't even have a story to tell the Quince . . ."

"Okay, okay, I give up," Lynn said, throwing her arms in the air. "You're right, it probably is a stupid idea to tell Quince anything. I don't know, though, I just have a weird feeling about this. Anyone skulking around in the middle of the night is up to no good."

"Hey, speak for yourself," Peter teased. "Seriously, though, I think something funny's going on, too. I did see lights on Mount Fear," he trailed off, seeing the skepticism in his friends' eyes.

Still, Shane could tell Lynn and Peter were both sort of

worried about the whole thing, even if it was for different reasons.

"Look, I don't really think there's anything to worry about, but let's keep our eyes open," he suggested. "Just in case Grat shows up again. Hey! We have to win the Winter Murals tomorrow. I don't know about you but I'm off to bed!"

"Me, too!" Lynn and Peter both said together. Peter laughed and as they turned to walk back to Apple House he threw his arm around Lynn's shoulder. "Don't worry, babe," he said in his tough detective voice. "Shane and me's gonna protect you from any Grat attack."

Lynn burst out laughing and wiggled away from his arm. She ran a few steps ahead and looked back at Peter. "More likely it'll be the other way around," she teased. "And I'll be saving you!"

CHAPTER 4

Lynn woke to the first glimmer of dawn and a silent house. The first thing she thought about was the cross-country ski race she had to win for Apple House. She threw back the covers, swung her feet over the side of the bed, and looked out the window.

The entire world was covered in at least a foot of fine, powdery snow! A lot more had fallen than the weatherman predicted. The fir trees spreading down the hills were drooping with great mounds of cotton-ball white. A thick blanket covered the roof of nearby Bear House. There was even a line of snow resting on the telephone wires. Big fat flakes still danced lazily in the air, and the sky was a uniform gray. It was impossible to tell if the weather would clear or get worse. Either way, with that kind of deep powder, Lynn knew it was going to be a great day for skiing.

Darlene was still fast asleep, so Lynn had the girls' bathroom to herself. She quickly dressed, and soon crept quietly down the stairs and out the front door. She

24

wanted to give the bottom of her skis one more coat of wax before the race.

The sun on the horizon spread its delicate pink rays across the snowy peaks of the forests. Everywhere Lynn looked was snow-covered. Her boots left the first imprints in the smooth powder.

She reached the new barn at the end of Sky Walk and saw the tractor clearing snow from the yard. The blade had been attached to the front, so it looked like a bulldozer pushing the snow into huge drifts. Just as Lynn turned toward the equipment shed where her skis were kept, someone shouted her name over the sound of the tractor's engine. She saw Shane waving to her from the cab of the tractor. Tiny, the maintenance man, was standing in the cab behind him.

"Tiny's showing me how to drive it!" Shane called to her as the tractor rumbled past, pushing a humongous pile of snow ahead of it. Shane was beaming with delight. As part of his daily chores at Northwood, Shane had been assigned to help out the maintenance man. Despite his name, Tiny was actually enormous, so big that from a distance, he even looked like Frankenstein.

Lynn waved. She was about to move on when she heard footsteps stomping through the snow behind her. She turned around and met the eyes of Thelonius Quincy, bundled up in an enormous gray parka with a fur-trimmed hood pulled tightly around his face. His bright blues lit up when he saw her.

"Up so early, Lynn!" the Quince piped up. "And how is my favorite cross-country skier!"

Lynn was momentarily taken aback by the compliment.

Quincy winked at her. "Well, I know I'm not supposed to show any favoritism," he said in almost a whisper, smiling secretively. "But you're a fine skier, and very good competition for Mark. You know, he's going to try very hard today to keep his record."

Lynn smiled. "I'm ready for him, sir. And so is the rest of Apple House! In fact, I got up early to give my skis another coat of wax."

The Quince beamed. "That's the Northwood spirit, Lynn! If someone were to ask me, I'd tell them you stood a good chance to win today."

"Really!" said Lynn, thrilled by the encouragement.

"Absolutely. Good luck!" With that, the Quince passed on, stomping his way toward the Lodge through the knee-high snow.

By the time Lynn finished waxing her skis, it was time for breakfast in the dining hall. That morning, it was a lot noisier than usual, and everyone seemed in a hurry to finish their oatmeal and head outside. Each house rallied around their team members for last-minute organizational details.

As everyone finished eating, all the kids in Raccoon House—they were wearing orange T-shirts with the house name on the front and back—jumped onto the benches at their table and began chanting a rap song they'd written for their team.

The kids from Mountain House were sitting next to them, and instantly jumped into the spirit. Soon the entire dining hall was pulsating with steady, rhythmic cheers and slogans as each house tried to outshout the other.

At the teachers' table, the Quince was looking around with a bemused smile, his eyes glowing with pride. Finally he stood, walked to the front of the cafeteria and raised his hands.

The slogans and chants and rap songs finished in a loud cheer, with the names of the houses being shouted out for the last time. Then it ended with laughter and sudden silence as the Quince stood to address Northwood's student body.

"The first race will be the cross-country," he said. "Followed by the toboggan race. Then we'll break for lunch and chores. In the afternoon, we'll start with the downhill ski race—and then the Tug-of-War to decide the winners. In between races, hot chocolate will be available outside the new barn—thanks to Miss Greyburne and Miss Pebbels, your music and art teachers." Mr. Quincy smiled broadly. "And one more surprise—for dessert tonight, there'll be hot fudge sundaes!"

At this news everyone cheered loudly. Sweet treats like this were rare at Northwood, which prided itself on its healthy diet. Lynn noticed that Shane looked disappointed. "What's the matter? You'd rather have tofu and granola?" she asked incredulously.

"I'm allergic to dairy," he groaned.

Lynn smiled. "Oh well, I don't like chocolate. But plain ice cream's fine with me."

◆ ◆ ◆

The cross-country ski race was on a mile-long course that led around the borders of Northwood. Unlike downhill skiing, where the racers started at the top of a hill and skied down, cross-country skiing was more like hiking or snowshoeing—except on skis. The course led up and down over hills in the forest. Going down a hill cross-country style was easy, but it was hard work to ski uphill. The skiers had to really use their poles, which was hard on arm muscles, and slide across the snow a certain way in order not to slip backward, which was hard on leg muscles. The cross-country ski race ended at the finish line in the field beside the big old Quincy house. The starting line was on the other side of the farm—where the course led into the forest behind the Lodge.

As the kids from Apple House marched toward the starting line, Jeff insisted on carrying Lynn's skis. "It's for Apple House," he assured her. "You gotta rest for the race." He hoisted her skis over his shoulder.

Darlene looke around to make sure no one was watching. Then she reached into her pocket and pulled out several small boxes of raisins and a milk chocolate bar. "I raided my stash for energy food." Darlene said, shoving them into the deep pockets of Lynn's ski jacket. "In case you get pooped out there on the trail."

"It's only a mile," Peter said, eyeing the chocolate bar with a hungry look in his eyes.

"I doubt I'll even have time to stop and open one," Lynn pointed out. "After all, it is a race."

"That's true!" Peter interjected. "And I could—"

"But thanks anyway," Lynn said quickly, patting the

bulge in her pocket. Candy and snacks were always good for barter if she didn't need them on the trail.

By the time Apple House's team arrived at the starting line, most of the school had assembled. Each house's students stood ready to cheer their teams on. The racers were buckling their skis on near the starting line, where the Quince stood, holding a bright, fluorescent signal flag.

The Apple House gang gave Lynn a rousing send-off. She buckled her boots into the skis.

"Good luck," Mrs. Durrell, their house counselor, said with an encouraging smile.

"Thanks," Lynn murmured. She waved to the rest of the house, and caught Shane watching her intently. He raised one hand, his thumb and index finger making a circle. Lynn hop-turned on her skis, dug the poles into the snow to push off, and sailed downhill to the starting line.

Since the trail was too narrow for everyone to go at once, the racers were staggered to take off one after the other, and different teachers had been appointed timers. They stood near the flags that marked the starting gate, holding stopwatches. Whoever reached the finish line in the shortest amount of time would be the winner.

The Quince paced back and forth, carrying the hand-held megaphone that he loved using for sports events.

"I hope I'm near the end," Lynn muttered to Shane.

Shane looked at her. "Why? I'd just as soon go first and get it over with."

Lynn wrinkled her nose. "First? Ugh."

Mr. Rapoport stood to one side with a clipboard in one

hand and his other holding the number vests. When Lynn reported to him, he told her she was number two.

Lynn sighed. "Just my luck. Who's first?" she asked.

"Mark Lepine for Crow," the math teacher told her. She walked back to Shane and Peter, holding the blue nylon vest with a giant number two on both sides.

"I'm second. Looks like I'll get it over with real fast." She laughed bravely, but it sounded hollow.

Shane helped her pull the number vest over her head and tied the front and back together with strings at the side. "You know why you're second after Lepine, don't you?" he asked her.

"No, why?"

"Because you and he are the fastest. To avoid logjams. The slower ones might be in the way of the skiers who are coming after them."

"So the Quince figures I'll have the second-best time?" Lynn asked, a little puzzled by what Shane was telling her.

Shane shook his head. "No, but he figures you're faster than everyone else—except maybe Mark."

"Just be careful," Darlene warned. "Don't wipe out."

"Are you kidding?" Lynn asked. "I'll be going so fast, I won't have time to."

The Quince's voice boomed through his megaphone across the snow-covered field, calling the racers to the starting line. The orange flag went down, and instantly Mark was off, his ski poles almost a blur as he dug them into the powder snow.

"This is it," Peter said matter-of-factly. "Watch out in case Grat is skulking in the woods."

Lynn and Shane both gave Peter withering looks.

Once again the Quince's voice boomed across the snowy field, this time calling Lynn's name. She slipped up to the starting line, which was marked by two aluminum poles with fluttering blue pennants. Mr. Lister, one of the English teachers, stood nearby holding a stopwatch. Lynn crouched in the starting position, and listened for the countdown. Mr. Lister simultaneously dropped his flag and clicked the watch.

Lynn was off!

The powder was so light she felt as if she were flying across the snow. The flakes danced like small white feathers in her wake. As she entered the deep pine forest, the cheers from the students and teachers faded into the silence of the great, still winter. Mark's tracks were clearly visible, carving lines through the perfect snow.

Lynn veered sharply around a twist in the trail on a downhill slope, making a wide turn to maintain her speed. The trail rose sharply. She hiked uphill, digging her poles into the snow to propel her forward. Soon, she could see Mark ahead of her through the trees, and felt her heart racing. It wasn't just because of the exertion of cross-country skiing. Despite Mark's one-minute head start, she was catching up!

She swung around another turn in the trail, just in time to see Mark's green hat bob below the crest of a hill. If she could gain momentum on this leg of the race, Lynn realized, she actually might overtake him!

She noticed Mark's trail veer sharply through the powder snow to the edge of the trail. That was odd, she thought. Why would Mark take the long way around in a race? No wonder he was losing time, the way he was zigzagging back and forth on a downhill run.

Once again she dug her poles hard into the snow and scissored her legs to propel her forward. Soon she was going exhilaratingly fast. Looking ahead to the bottom of the hill, she saw the trail curving gradually to the right. She flexed her ankles, turning her skis slightly onto the edges to get ready for the curve.

Suddenly, she felt something hard beneath her skis. The deep powder flew up in a flurry of snowflakes. The front of her skis caught on something, making a grinding sound of wood scratching against rocks. Before she could even react, Lynn slammed to a stop and flew head over heels, tumbling through the air in a dangerous tangle of skis, poles, arms, and legs!

CHAPTER 5

Lynn hit the ground hard, and lay perfectly still for a moment. She felt a dull ache spreading through her back where she had landed. She was so tangled up, she had to think to figure out where her arms and legs were. One by one, she tested each limb, and was relieved to find nothing broken. She pulled her wrists from the leather loops at the tops of her poles, and slowly untangled her skis. The safety release on the buckles had given, so she buckled her boots back into the harness. Then she grabbed her ski poles and used them to push herself to her feet.

"Darn," she muttered, her mind only on the race. She'd lost at least 30 seconds from her time. She looked down quickly to see what had caused the wipeout.

Rocks! There was a pile of them in the middle of the trail. They'd been totally concealed by the newly fallen snow. Mark's tracks had narrowly avoided them, but Lynn had skied right down the middle. *How did they get there?* Lynn wondered. She'd skied down the trail for practice dozens of times. They definitely hadn't been there a few days earlier.

"I don't have time to figure this out right now," she muttered angrily, aware that each second ticking away was spoiling her chances of winning the race.

She pushed off, and was quickly back up to speed, pulling into the finish line less than a minute later. All the kids in Apple House were cheering madly as she skied across the final stretch. Mr. Lister's flag came down, and Miss Bennet called out her time.

Eight minutes and forty-two seconds!

Lynn winced. It was good, but not great. Those rocks had really held her up. Not far away, she saw Mark, smiling happily and surrounded by the other kids in Crow House.

"Congratulations!" Shane told her, when her friends ran over to her.

"That was really good!" Darlene announced, unable to hide the disappointment in her voice.

"But not good enough," Jeff said sympathetically. "Mark Lepine came in at eight minutes and fifteen seconds."

"Darn, if it hadn't been for those rocks in the trail—" Lynn started to say angrily.

"What rocks?" Peter demanded.

"I wiped out," Lynn told him. "There's a pile of rocks right in the middle of the trail, and they were hidden by the snow."

"That's impossible," Jeff said. "I was one of the people who cleared that trail last November before the snow fell.

We made sure it was cleared of rocks and stumps and stuff.''

"Tell me about it," Lynn said grimly. "I've skied that trail dozens of times in the past week and they weren't there then, either. But they're there now," Lynn went on. "And my spill cost me just enough time for Mark to win."

"Didn't Mark hit the rocks, too?" Darlene asked.

Lynn shook her head. "Almost, I think. But his tracks were just to one side. He was lucky."

"Lucky, my butt," Peter snorted. "He probably put them there."

Shane looked at Peter skeptically. "Give me a break, Peter. Why would he do that?"

"So he could win!" Peter exclaimed.

"Well, you shouldn't make accusations like that unless you have proof," Lynn told him firmly. "I can't believe anyone, especially Mark, would be so unsporting."

"Peter has a suspicious mind," Darlene teased. "First he sees a ghost, then he thinks old man Grat is ready to attack Northwood any second, and now he's accusing Mark of things."

Peter reddened and was about to protest when Shane spoke up. "We'll just have to win the other three events," he said with determination.

Serge Williams naturally couldn't resist coming over to gloat. "Face it, losers, Crow has the Winter Murals wrapped up for the third year in a row," he taunted, "so why don't you guys take a break and go home now?"

"Yeah, right. Scared we'll show you up if we stay, huh?" Peter shot back.

"Dream on, fat boy!" Serge shouted. Priscilla came up behind him to add her own jeers.

"Apple House is apple sauce," she sneered. "You guys are gonna lose!"

"I bet my sundae we don't!" Peter said boldly.

"You're on!" Serge snarled.

"Yeah," Priscilla seconded. "I'll bet mine, too."

Peter was nonplussed for a second. "I can't bet two sundaes," he said. "I only have one."

"Well I'll bet mine that we win," Lynn said quickly.

"And I'll bet mine, too," Shane added.

Soon, a bunch of kids had gathered around. They chose sides, and by the time they finished making their deals, everyone had bet their sundaes on either Apple House or Crow House.

Suddenly, the Quince's voice boomed through his megaphone. He announced that Mark Lepine was the winner of the cross-country ski race, with Lynn second.

Lynn looked at her housemates and shrugged.

"Bad break," Shane said sympathetically, throwing his arm around her shoulders and giving her a quick hug. "If those rocks hadn't been there, you'd have won."

Jeff and Darlene looked glum, and an awkward silence fell among the friends.

The Quince's amplified voice floated in the background, announcing the next event.

Peter brightened. "Don't worry, Apples, I've got the toboggan race all wrapped up. In fact, they should just forget the race and announce Apple House the winner."

"Yeah?" Darlene said, obviously a little doubtful.

Peter just smiled wider and patted his plump sides. "All year round I've been working on extra weight for this. You wait and see," he concluded confidently. He turned to Shane and Lynn. "Ready?" he asked. He led the group to the toboggan run on Mount Lookout.

Outside the toboggan shed, halfway up the slope, they found Miss Greyburne and Miss Pebbels, clad in wool caps and mittens, ladling hot chocolate from a steaming stainless-steel vat to an enthusiastic line of kids. Other kids were straggling up the slopes of Mount Lookout. The snow had stopped completely, and the gray sky had lightened.

"Smells like more snow," Jeff said.

Shane looked at him as they joined the crowd streaming up the hill toward the toboggan run. "What does?"

"The air," Jeff told him. Shane watched his nostrils flare. Jeff sniffed, as if he caught a scent wafting through it. "It's hard to explain," he told Shane. Shane looked at him, baffled.

"It smells frosty, sort of. I don't know." Jeff laughed with obvious exasperation. "I grew up in North Bay in Ontario. I've been smelling that smell all my life. And to me, it smells like there's going to be more snow."

"That's why there were ghost lights on Mount Fear last night," Peter interjected.

Darlene rolled her eyes. "Get off it, Peter!" she said, annoyed.

Shane just shook his head. The air smelled perfectly normal to him. Just cold. And the sky was definitely getting lighter. "Tell you what, Peter. If I'm wrong and it does snow, you can have my dessert tonight. If I'm right I win two desserts from you."

"I thought you didn't eat dairy."

"I don't. But I can trade them for something else."

Peter nodded, a sly smile spreading across his face. He looked at Jeff, then up at the sky. "Deal."

They claimed their toboggan at the shed, a six-foot-long cedar strip called *Arrow Mohawk*. Even though Northwood had a supply of toboggans for everyone to use, the students were also allowed to bring their own. Peter's dad had given him the *Arrow Mohawk* for Christmas. It was sleek and narrow, with the polished wood curled up at the front, and red nylon reins looped along the sides.

Quince announced the beginning of the race. All the teams lined up along the crest of the toboggan hill, a thousand-foot-long slope that curved gently down to the valley. The sides of the run had been carefully lined with high snowdrifts that had been evenly sprayed with water. The water froze into a solid ice shell, forming a barrier to keep the tobogganers from veering off into the woods and crashing against a tree. Some moguls—round bumps of ice and snow—were scattered here and there on the slope, but they were all fairly low and gentle. The most they could do was slow the toboggan down.

Peter took the reins in front and tucked his feet under the curving headboard. Lynn piled on behind him. She pushed her boots under his knees, and held tightly to his ample waist. Shane got on behind Lynn. He looked along the crest of the hill at the other teams waiting at the starting line. Mark, Serge, and Priscilla from Crow House were teamed together three toboggans over.

Mark turned suddenly, catching Shane's eyes. Slowly, without taking his eyes away, he smiled a smile of serene confidence.

Darlene and Jeff came up on each side of Shane. "Ready for the push-off?" Darlene asked.

"Ready as we'll ever be," Shane muttered. He felt Darlene and Jeff place their hands firmly on his back. They dug their heels into the snow.

"On the count of three," the Quince boomed, beginning the countdown. "One."

"Just don't go over Dead Man's Shortcut," Jeff cautioned, almost as an afterthought.

"Dead Man's Shortcut?" Shane asked, suddenly a little worried.

Jeff nodded. "It's a chasm near the end of the run. If you get across it you can knock at least a minute off your time."

"Two!" the Quince's megaphoned voice announced.

"If?" Shane asked, with a sensation of dread.

"No sweat," Peter chimed in from the front of the toboggan. "We'll be so far ahead by that time we can take the long way around and it won't make a difference."

The sharp report of the starter's pistol shattered the winter air. With loud grunts, Darlene and Jeff pushed, and Shane felt the toboggan surging forward. Peter let out a shrill whoop, that Lynn imitated, and then Shane. The toboggan picked up speed and was zinging down the sharp incline. The cold air whistled past Shane's eyes, whipping his hair away from his face.

"*Whoooooooeeee!*" Peter whooped again. Toboggans were speeding downhill from one side to the other. Apple House was a good toboggan's length ahead, when suddenly Hill House's team caught a vein of smooth ice and surged past them at tremendous speed.

Peter watched them sail effortlessly ahead in disbelief. Then he saw a small round hill, like a giant bump, coming at them. "Mogul!" he yelled at the top of his lungs. "Lean left!"

Shane and Lynn immediately shifted their weight. Peter pulled frantically at the reins, tugging hard on the right side. The toboggan began to edge sideways across the hill. Narrowly, they avoided the mogul.

"Steady!" Peter yelled, shifting his weight back to the center of the toboggan and pulling on the left rein. Shane and Lynn followed. The toboggan straightened, and picked up speed again. The run was turned in a long, gentle curve, banked by snow. Beyond, the forest of fir trees grew to the edge, intersected by craggy faces of rock.

Peter allowed himself a quick glance along the hill. The toboggans from two other houses had pulled ahead. But the Crow House team was nowhere to be seen. Peter turned back to the hill, just in time to see one of the lead toboggans catch a bad angle and wipe out against another mogul, spilling its team across the snow. They scrambled to right their toboggan and get back on. Peter felt his pulse quicken. Mark Lepine and Serge Williams were somewhere way behind them. He was going to win!

"Mogul!" he heard Shane shout, seeing the rise coming at them at the same time.

"Lean right!" Peter shouted. This time he pulled hard on the left rein.

And it broke.

Peter's body jerked back with the sudden release of tension, falling against Lynn, and pushing her back into Shane. The mogul was coming up at them fast.

"I can't steer!" Peter screamed. He felt the toboggan starting to spin sideways, and hunched forward over the curving headboard to slow it.

"Wipe out!" Lynn shouted.

Something on one side moved rapidly into Peter's peripheral vision just as the toboggan hit the mogul and slipped out from underneath them. Mark Lepine whizzed past on the Crow toboggan, heading for the finish line.

CHAPTER 6

The three teammates from Apple House tumbled into the deep snow, while the toboggan pitched downhill. Peter grabbed the single rein that still held and gripped hard. The toboggan jerked to a stop on the hillside, pulling Peter slowly after it. He turned on his side and dug his heels into the snow. Quickly, Lynn was beside him, pulling the toboggan back. Toboggans from other houses were whizzing past them on both sides, their riders hooting at the fallen teammates. Several hundred yards further downhill, another house wiped out on a mogul, spilling the players into the snow.

"Quick, Shane! Give me your belt!" Peter ordered, pulling the toboggan under him. He tied the broken end off on the cord that ran around the toboggan's frame.

Shane looked baffled. Then he caught on, and quickly unbuckled and tore his leather belt from the loops around his waist. Peter took it, wrapped it around the remaining

42

cord, and buckled it closed. He gripped it with both hands—a perfectly improvised set of reins. "All aboard!" he shouted. Lynn and Shane piled on, pushing off first to gain a strong starting speed.

They whipped past the team from Mountain House who'd spilled just below them. They'd lost their toboggan completely. Dispiritedly, they were searching for it in the powdered snow, farther downhill at the edge of the forest.

"We'll never win!" Shane shouted into the cold wind stinging past his cheeks.

"Yes, we will!" Peter called back.

"No way!"

Lynn turned her head. "Way! We've gotta take Dead Man's Shortcut!"

"Lean right!" Peter pulled the belt tightly on the left side and adjusted his weight for a left turn.

"Oh noooo!" Shane screamed when he saw where they were headed. The slope dropped steeply—it seemed almost vertical—and ended abruptly at a precipice and thin air.

Even though he had done it three times before—twice in his first year at Northwood, and once last year—Peter still had to close his eyes. He felt the snowy slope give way to pure sky beneath the wooden boards, followed by a moment of eerie silence.

Then he felt the bottom of the sled slam into the snow with a loud *whomp*, and slide even faster. He opened his eyes. Far uphill on his right, the first toboggans slid into view around the curving slope, still several hundred yards away. Straight ahead of them by a hundred feet was the finish line.

"*Yeeehawww!*" Peter screamed like a cowboy.

"Cool," Shane murmured, with half a smile stretching across his amazed face. He realized he was clutching Lynn tightly and she had her face buried in Peter's back. A quick glance over his shoulder told him about Dead Man's Shortcut, a place where the mountain slope was cut by a deep ravine. The slope below was steep, and the gap over the chasm was five or six feet. But it was a direct run to the finish line, for those who were brave—or foolhardy—enough to try it.

"There's Crow," Lynn warned loudly. Shane turned in time to see the toboggan carrying Mark, Serge, and Priscilla coming up behind them and moving fast.

"They're gaining!" Shane shouted.

"Lean forward more!" Peter ordered, bending his weight over the bowed front of the toboggan. Shane and Lynn shifted forward, leaning hard into Peter. In his side vision, Shane saw the front of Crow's toboggan gaining steadily.

Suddenly, Peter, Lynn, and Shane heard the deafening roar of cheers. Peter straightened up just as the toboggan tore beneath the long green banner and across the finish line. They started slowing on the level soccer field at the end of the toboggan run. As Crow pulled up beside them, Mark glared at them.

"Way to go!" Jeff shouted, running up to the toboggan with Darlene right behind him. Peter, Lynn, and Shane rose shakily to their feet, brushing snow from their nylon ski coats and pants. Quickly, the Apple House team was surrounded by friends and housemates, shouting cheers and congratulations.

Suddenly, Serge's loud, belligerent voice broke through the sounds of the crowd. "No fair! No fair—they cheated!"

"Did not!" Peter retorted loudly. "The fastest toboggan run down Mount Lookout wins—and Dead Man's Shortcut is part of the mountain."

All heads turned when the Quince started across the snow-covered soccer field, with Mr. Rapoport and Mr. and Mrs. Durrell in tow. When Serge saw the headmaster approaching, he turned to him and repeated his accusations. Someone in the crowd—Shane thought it might have been Jeff—shouted out that Serge was crazy.

"We won by the rules," Peter said with certainty, addressing his statement to the Quince. "Besides, our rope broke and we wiped out because of that. We needed to save time."

"Oh, yeah. Sure!" Serge groaned.

Mr. Quincy put up his hands to quiet everyone. Then he took the small, dog-eared notebook from his pocket, and began to read. "The winner of the toboggan race shall be the team that descends Mount Lookout in the shortest possible time." He looked around at the gathered students. Then he motioned toward the slope of Mount Lookout. "To be perfectly honest, Dead Man's Shortcut is really too risky for anyone to be using."

A troubled silence fell over the crowd of well-wishers. The Quince continued. "But for the time being, Peter is right. I declare Apple House the winner of the toboggan run!"

A giant cheer erupted from the gathered students, and Peter felt hands pulling at him. Suddenly he was hoisted into the air and onto the shoulders of his housemates.

"Lunch will be served in ten minutes!" the Quince called over the exuberant noise.

As Northwood's students marched off to the dining hall, Shane dropped behind and ran back to the toboggan. He knelt and began to unbuckle his belt from the front. He heard someone behind him. He swung around. It was Lynn.

"Sorry," she said. "Didn't mean to startle you. I thought you might want help taking the toboggan back."

"Sure," Shane smiled, standing. "Let's go."

They crossed the soccer field and headed up the path that led to the toboggan shed. On the way, they both shared their memories from the amazing toboggan race—especially the leap over Dead Man's Shortcut.

"I always wanted to do it," Lynn admitted. "But I was always too chicken to lead the way."

Shane laughed. "Trust Peter to be crazy enough to actually go for it." He looked at Lynn. "It was kind of fun," he admitted.

They came to the shed, set in a snow-filled clearing surrounded by birch trees. The big double doors were open, exposing the racks where various sleds and toboggans were hanging. Shane lifted Peter's *Arrow Mohawk*. He was about to hang it beside the others when he noticed the broken rope.

"Look at this," he said quietly, holding up the broken end for Lynn to see.

"What about it?" Lynn asked, looking curiously at the frayed end.

"It was done with a knife," Shane said. He pointed to the break. The nylon fibers around the outside of the rope were neatly severed. Only the center strands had pulled and frayed apart. "Someone cut the rope all the way around, leaving only a little bit to hold it together—until Peter started tugging on it to steer."

"You mean, someone did this deliberately?" Lynn asked, surprised. "But who?" Then it struck her. "We saw someone skulking around up here last night."

Shane nodded. "Someone wearing a red coat." Shane looked down at the clipped rope from the toboggan. "It's like someone deliberately tried to sabotage us in the event."

"And what about the rocks on the ski trail this morning?" Lynn asked suddenly. "They weren't there before, I'm sure of it."

"Jeff was pretty sure of that, too," Shane agreed. "That means someone put them there last night, knowing the snow would hide them."

"Along with their tracks," Lynn pointed out.

Shane looked through the woods to the other side of Mount Lookout, where the orange flags for the finish line of the cross-country ski race flapped and snapped in the zero-degree breeze.

"Say, can you show me where those rocks are?" Shane asked. "We should go have a look at them."

CHAPTER 7

Shane and Lynn waded through knee-high powder, cutting through the forest until they came to the bright pink flags that marked the finish line. Here the field of snow had been trampled flat by all the kids and teachers who had been watching.

They started walking back up the ski trail. A dozen pairs of skis, zigzagging their way along the final stretch, had packed the snow down. This made the going a lot easier than it would have been otherwise, even though Shane and Lynn still struggled uphill on foot. The exertion made them pant, and soon great clouds of steam emerged in the cold air whenever they exhaled.

"Over there," Lynn said finally, when they climbed a curve and saw a pile of football-sized boulders sticking up through the snow in the middle of the hill. All the signs—including a pair of broken and abandoned skis—indicated that other skiers had met the same fate as Lynn.

"You think someone put them there last night?" Lynn asked.

Shane shrugged and looked around. So many people had been through there that the lower branches of the pine trees lining the trail had been brushed free of snow. But in the forest beyond, he noted, the snow was completely undisturbed beneath the heavy branches. The pile of rocks in the middle of the trail had been almost completely cleared of snow by colliding skiers.

"There's snow underneath those rocks," Shane pointed out. "That means they were put there after the last snowfall."

"That was a couple of weeks ago," Lynn recalled. "It was snowing the day everyone came back after Christmas vacation."

Shane smiled. "That was the day I started at Northwood. I'll never forget. I felt like my parents had sent me to Siberia."

"Do you still feel that way?" Lynn asked, astonished at her own boldness.

Shane looked at her. He liked her blue eyes, and the way she spoke up and said what was on her mind all the time. Not to mention that like him, she was a good athlete and a tough competitor.

He smiled. "Yeah, it still feels like Siberia. But I've moved around a lot because my dad's an engineer and he works in foreign countries. And I think I made friends here at Northwood faster than anywhere else. Like you."

He waded to the edge of the trail and crossed into the forest, peering closely at the snow.

"What are you doing?" Lynn asked, watching him go.

"Looking for tracks," he called back to her. "If someone put those stones there, they must have carried them from the forest.''

''But it snowed,'' she pointed out. ''Any tracks would be covered.''

Taking wide steps, Shane strode into the forest, his legs sinking in over his knees in the deep drifts that covered the forest floor. He pulled himself along using the thin, smooth trunks of moose maple trees—which grew like giant weeds in the Adirondack forests—until he reached the canopy of pine trees. The snow cover on the ground there was much thinner. Very little snow could filter down through the branches of fifty-foot-high white pines. In places, the wind had even swept the forest floor bare, exposing frozen heaps of brown pine needles.

In the shadows cast by the overhead branches, still visible and frozen into the surface of the snow, was the giant imprint of a snowshoe!

''I found one,'' Shane called excitedly.

Lynn struggled through the snow and knelt beside him. ''It's just like the ones we saw at the toboggan shed last night.''

They walked back to the trail. Shane stood near the half-buried pile of rocks and looked around one last time. His eye caught something in the snow, near the edge of the trail. It was red, like blood against the white snow.

He reached into the snow and felt something hard and flat. He pulled his hand out and held up a red hunter's cap. It was definitely the same one that Grat had been wearing when he invaded the dining hall the day before.

''A Grat attack,'' Lynn concluded, staring at the red hat.

"But if it's Grat, why's he doing it?" Shane asked. "I mean, what does he have to gain?"

"To get back at the Quince?" Lynn suggested. "The Quincy family and the Grats have been enemies for about two hundred years, ever since the Grats accused Benjamin Quincy of pushing Martin Grat off Mount Fear. And you saw Grat last night in the cafeteria. He's crazy. Maybe he decided it was time to get revenge. If kids here started having terrible accidents, it would give Northwood a bad name. Our parents would send us to a different school."

Shane nodded. "Maybe that's Grat's plan—to close down Northwood. It could work, too. If he keeps this up, someone could get hurt."

"Or worse," Lynn added ominously.

They walked back to the main campus together. Shane noticed that the heavy gray sky had grown darker again. "Looks like it's going to snow again," he commented. "Guess Peter won my sundae."

A strong breeze blew down from Mount Fear, whipping the ends of Lynn's scarf. She felt the icy chill seeping through her heavy winter clothing. "It's supposed to clear," she said, hopefully. She added before she could stop herself, " 'Course, Peter saw the ghost lights on Mount Fear last night. That means there's going to be a major blizzard."

Shane looked doubtfully at her. "You really believe all that ghost stuff? Or have you been talking to Peter too much?"

Lynn felt embarrassed. "I dunno," she said casually. "I guess it's just a story."

51

When they arrived at the dining hall, Peter was basking in his glory. Shane and Lynn sat down at the table in time to hear him remind everyone who bet against him that they each owed him their sundae at dinner that night.

"Fourteen sundaes to collect tonight," Peter announced. "Including yours, Shane, because it's started snowing again." He pointed out the window where fat, sparkly snowflakes floated lazily in the air. " 'Course if you want your dessert back, I wouldn't mind trading for that new CD you got—"

"No way, Peter," Shane told him. "I'm allergic to dairy products, remember? And I'd rather keep the CD."

Peter immediately turned to Lynn.

"Don't even ask, Peter," she said quickly. "Even if I don't like chocolate fudge sauce, I love ice cream and I plan on eating my sundae all by myself. By the way, Shane and I have some news about our toboggan accident when the rope broke."

"It didn't break," Shane told the kids from the Apple House. "It was cut. You can tell by looking at the rope."

"Shane found some snowshoe tracks, too," Lynn said. "The same ones we saw last night outside the shed—only up where those rocks were piled on the cross-country trail. I think old man Grat is trying to wreck the Winter Murals."

"Grat attacks," Peter said in a low, ominous voice.

"But why?" Darlene asked.

"Maybe if a Northwood student gets hurt, the school will get a bad reputation and have to close," Lynn suggested.

"He wants revenge because Ben Quincy murdered his ancestor," Peter said.

Lynn looked at Peter, her face twisted with annoyance. "That's not true," she insisted. "Martin Grat slipped and fell off Mount Fear. He wasn't pushed."

"Then why is Ben Quincy's ghost walking around up there?" Peter argued.

"There aren't any ghosts up there, Peter," Lynn said angrily.

"There are, too," Peter maintained, his voice growing louder. "I saw it last Halloween when Serge and I climbed up Mount Fear to dangle lights from the ledge. And I saw the ghost of Ben Quincy, not Martin Grat! I don't care if you don't believe me because I know it's true!"

Lynn looked thoroughly exasperated. "It wasn't a real ghost, Peter. It was just some other kids from Northwood who went up there to scare you and Serge."

Tight-lipped, Peter shook his head emphatically. "This was a real ghost," he persisted. "And it was Ben Quincy's ghost."

Shane decided to break up the argument. "It doesn't matter if there's a ghost on Mount Fear or not," he pointed out. "Someone real—probably Grat—is trying to sabotage the Winter Murals, and someone might get hurt."

"We should check the downhill slope for rocks before the next ski race," Jeff suggested. Around the table, heads nodded. Darlene, Jeff, and Delia volunteered to give the slope the once-over.

Just then, Mark Lepine passed by carrying a tray of salad stuff. He kept himself on a special diet because he had skin problems. He was teased about it sometimes, and called Granola Man. As he went by, he taunted Lynn, "Too bad you couldn't beat me in the cross-country ski race. Maybe you need a better strategy."

"Give me a break, Pizza Face," Lynn muttered under her breath.

Shane stood up and turned toward the class president. "You don't need strategy, Mark, you need skill," he said confidently. "And I'll win this afternoon because I have what it takes."

Mark laughed. "Oh yeah, right, it's the new kid from Filthy-delphia."

Shane felt a flash of anger surge through him. He stepped closer to Mark. "Oh yeah?"

Just then, a blast of cold air entered as Tiny, the maintenance man, came inside. He went to the counselors' table and whispered a few words to the Quince. A moment later, the headmaster rose and addressed his students.

"It would seem that the weatherman has been caught short," he began. "Tiny has just informed me that up to twelve inches of snow may fall by tomorrow morning."

"See, a storm *is* coming," Peter whispered to his table. "I told you I saw ghost lights on Mount Fear last night!"

CHAPTER 8

By the time the next event in the Winter Murals began—
the downhill ski race—the snow was falling hard, the tiny
frozen flakes swirled by the icy north wind.

"Everyone's betting on Mark to win," Jeff said, trot-
ting along beside Darlene and Peter. They were walking
Shane to the ski lift on Morning Peak.

"Well, everyone knows he's the best skier," Darlene
said as if to explain. She quickly added, " 'Course, the
other kids haven't seen how good a skier Shane is."

Peter slugged Shane lightly on the shoulder. "You
know I won fourteen sundaes on the toboggan race and
guess what—I bet twelve of them on you winning."

Shane caught sight of little pink flags fluttering from
the finish line. Already another layer of powder snow was
accumulating over what had fallen the night before. The
other racers were lining up at the ski tow, where Mr.
Benson and Mr. Rapoport watched.

The ski tow was called a T-bar. Two long thick cables

had been strung on high, steel towers running down the side of Morning Peak. Dangling from the cables were aluminum T-bars—they looked like upside-down T's. At the bottom of the ski hill, a little shed housed the machinery that ran the lift. An engine wound the long cables around and around, so the T-bars were pulled a thousand feet up the side of Morning Peak to the starting line. The T-bars going up the mountain each held two skiers. Since everyone skied down, the T-bars coming down the mountain and back into the shed were empty.

The downhill ski run was almost half a mile long, and Shane had been practicing on it ever since he'd arrived at Northwood. Parts of it were steep, but there were also flat stretches and some parts that were heavily moguled. The last two hundred feet were really steep, and straight downhill to the finish line.

The kids from Apple House arrived at the lift, and watched one of the T-bars pull out. The way this T-bar worked, as the cable moved forward, each end of the inverted metal T caught two skiers lightly, and began to draw them up the hill. Two more skiers stepped in place, and another T-bar began to move forward with the cable.

"This is it," Shane said, turning to the kids in his house.

"Break a leg, dude!" Jeff said with enthusiasm. He added quickly, "That's what they say for good luck in the theater."

Shane got his number—five—from Mr. Rapoport. He pulled it over his head and tied it at the waist. Then he put on his skis. He stepped into line, and waited for his turn at the T-bar. The other kids waited beside him, following Shane as he shuffled forward in line.

Mark was just ahead of him, surrounded by skiers from other houses. He turned and saw Shane.

"Hey, anyone wants a second helping of dessert tonight, try betting with Apple House. They're all betting on their hero, and he's going to lose!"

"Just ignore him," Lynn murmured.

Other kids started turning to look in Shane's direction. Quickly, Peter started negotiating with Darlene, Jeff, and Delia for their desserts. The Raccoon House kids started betting on Mark, with Serge egging them on, and even writing their names on a little list he was keeping. Another T-bar left the shed and the cable pulled it uphill, carrying Mark away. Shane was next in line, with the skier from Raccoon House, a tall kid with dark brown hair named Keir Woodward.

Shane and Keir caught the T-bar. The cable tugged, and they began to slide up the side of Morning Peak.

At the top of the hill, the racers were taking up their positions by the starting line. As Shane skied into place, Mark pushed past him, flicking snow across Shane's skis. "Dude, I'm going to wipe you out," he called out.

"Yeah, just call me the King of Wipeouts," Shane retorted. "As in—wiping your record out of the Honor Roll."

Mark's face hardened, and he eyed Shane fiercely. Shane turned and put himself in position, bending his knees slightly, and aiming his skis down the hill. He scouted for a route between moguls, and eyed the inside of a curve in the run. The Quince's starter pistol sounded, and he pushed off.

Shane felt a rush of exhilaration in the cold wind. The featureless white hillside moved toward him at tremendous speed. His body went into automatic pilot, his knees absorbing the shape of the hill, pushing off the sides of moguls. Soon he realized he was ahead. Then, to his left he saw Mark, cutting back and forth down the steepest part of the slope. He was going so fast he was sometimes indistinguishable from the waves of powdery snow the flew up from his skis.

Shane cut sharply to the left to avoid another mogul. At the same instant he heard a harsh scraping sound. He felt his skis hit ice beneath the powdery snow. He started losing control. Mark, was coming down the hill right after him. Suddenly he saw Shane and tried to change direction.

The same scraping noise cut the air. Mark hit the ice patch and lost control, too, his poles flailing. Shane realized it too late to get out of the way. The two boys crashed together and went down, in a giant tangle of arms, legs, and skis. They rolled along the steep slope, while other skiers whipped past, some narrowly avoiding becoming part of the collision themselves.

When they stopped rolling, Shane and Mark were in the snow.

"You jerk!" Mark screamed at Shane. "You made me lose this race!"

They tried to break apart, but first were forced to separate their legs and skis, one limb at a time. When he was extricated from Shane, Mark snapped his boots back into the harnesses and pushed himself up. "I had this event sewn up! It was mine and you messed it up for me—"

By now, Mark and Shane were alone on the slope. All the other skiers had passed them and were probably nearing the finish line. When Shane tried to get up, Mark turned angrily and pushed him back down. Shane fell back in the snow.

"Hey, dude, chill!" Shane shouted at him. "It's just a race!"

"For you maybe, but not for me," Mark hissed, clenching his teeth. "I'm getting my name up on the Honor Roll for the third year in a row, and no one's going to stop me!"

Mark turned on his skis and pushed off, rapidly descending the hill. Shane sat back and watched him go. "It's only a game," he muttered quietly, brushing snow from his parka and pushing himself to his feet again.

By the time Shane pulled up to the finish line, hardly anyone was left to see him. Mr. Rapoport clicked off a stopwatch as he went past, but all the other kids were gathered in a crowd around the Quince. Northwood's headmaster was holding Keir Woodward's hand in the air in a gesture of victory. The kids—especially from Raccoon House—cheered loudly for the winner.

A moment later, Shane heard Lynn calling him. He turned and saw the other Apple House kids running over.

"What happened, dude?" Peter wailed.

Shane felt really awful. "Sorry, guys. Mark and I hit some ice and crashed up there.

"I saw Mark ski in really late and he looked lethal," Darlene commented. "He crossed the finish line and didn't even stop."

Shane shook his head in exasperation. "We both spilled. After that neither of us had a chance. Mark got really weird about it, though. He went ballistic, yelling at me and everything. I told him it's only a race. He takes it too seriously."

"I bet fourteen desserts on you," Peter said morosely.

Shane was barely able to suppress a smile. "There was nothing I could do," he said. "I'm real sorry about losing, guys."

"Forget it!" Peter told them. "Since a different house won each event, the Tug-of-War will be the eliminator. Raccoon versus Apple versus Crow House. But I'll tell you guys one thing: Mark Lepine's chances at his third year on the Honor Roll are starting to look totally slim."

CHAPTER 9

With twenty minutes to spare before the last event of the Winter Murals—the Tug-of-War—the kids found Miss Greyburne and Miss Pebbels had set up their hot-chocolate concession in front of the new barn, where the game was going to be played. As a special treat, the cook had sent over pots of hot maple toffee from last year's maple sugar season, when the students had gathered sap and boiled it down in the newly built maple-sugar shed.

Everyone helped themselves to a paper plate that they filled with fresh snow. Then Miss Greyburne poured a ladle of hot maple toffee over it. The toffee congealed instantly on the snow, and the kids ate it with wooden sticks, twirling the hardening toffee around them and lifting it to their mouths.

Although it was still only mid-afternoon, the sky had continued to darken until it almost seemed like dusk. It was snowing harder all the time.

"I hope we get this Tug-of-War over with soon," someone complained. "This is turning into a storm."

"Blizzard, more likely," Jeff said quietly, so just the other kids in Apple House heard. Then, from the crowd lined up to get more hot chocolate, Shane heard someone shout.

"Look up there! A light on Mount Fear!"

There was a momentary silence. Everyone turned to face the great dark mountain that towered over the valley like a jagged tooth. Then there was a hubbub of noise.

"I don't see anything," Darlene said.

"Me, neither," Lynn agreed.

"I can't see a light right now," Peter said, peering up at Mount Fear. "But I swear I saw one last night. Now do you believe me?"

Shane gave Peter a skeptical look. "Someone's climbed up there and whoever it is is waving a light from the ledge. That's all."

"In a blizzard? That's impossible," Peter insisted.

"Why?" Shane demanded. "You and Serge tried to do it last Halloween just to scare people. Maybe old man Grat is up there right now, waving a flashlight around."

"No way," Peter said. "That ledge up there is only about a foot wide, and it's even broken away in the middle. It's way too dangerous—especially for a fat old guy like Grat. Besides, even if someone does climb up there and flash lights, it doesn't explain the ghost I saw."

Lynn rolled her eyes. "I wish you'd stop with this ghost thing, Peter. No one believes you."

Before Peter could respond, Mr. Rapoport and Mr. Durrell came out of the barn carrying an enormous rope. It was nearly as thick as Shane's arm, and about fifty feet long. Shane watched them lay it on the ground in front of the barn, where the snow had been cleared by the tractor. Mr. Rapoport carefully paced off the length, and tied a bright red handkerchief exactly halfway down. Mr. Benson walked across the snow drawing a long straight line with blue chalk powder.

Peter and Lynn called Apple House together for a last quick strategy session.

"I'll be last man on the rope," Peter announced. "Because I'm the heaviest."

"Why's that so important?" Darlene wanted to know.

"I'll be like an anchor at our end of the rope. It'll make it harder for them to pull us across the line."

"Peter's right," Shane said. "And I know some good tug-of-war tricks, too."

"Neat," Lynn said.

"First, it's good for us to have something to chant so we all tug at the same time. Like if we all yell 'Tug the rope, tug the rope,' over and over like that, and each time we say 'tug' everyone tugs together."

"Like getting a cadence in bicycle racing," Jeff said. When he saw Peter looking at him, he explained, "If you develop a rhythm, you have more stamina."

"Too much," Peter muttered.

"Wait, I know another good trick," Shane continued. He lowered his voice until he was almost speaking in a whisper. "When I give you a signal, everyone has to let go of the rope—just for a split second. It'll throw the other team off balance for a moment. That's when we grab it again, and pull hard—real hard."

"And right across the line," Peter laughed.

"Excellent," Jeff exclaimed. "So what will be the signal?"

Shane thought for a moment. "We should be saying 'tug the rope' during a tug-of-war," he said slowly. "So when I yell 'tug *harder*'—that's when I want you to give them some slack instead!"

Once again the Quince's voice summoned the contestants. There were three houses competing—Apple, Crow, and Raccoon—because each of their teams had won a single Winter Mural event. "The winner of the first round," the Quince continued, "will play the third team, and the winner of that round wins the Quincy Cup!"

Peter, Mark, and Keir—the three winners of the day— met to pull straws. A hush fell over the crowd as each of the boys pulled his choice from Mr. Rapoport's closed hand. Although only three houses were competing, all the other houses had chosen sides. Mountain House and High House were rooting for Apple, but Moose House supported Crow, because one of Mark's friends lived there. Raccoon House was on its own, but the houses that supported Apple had loudly announced that their second choice was for Raccoon to win the trophy.

The three boys held up their straws. Mr. Rapoport and the Quince conferred quietly. The Quince raised his megaphone to his mouth and announced the results.

"In the first round, Crow House—"

His words were interrupted by cheers from the kids in Crow House and Moose House.

"The Crows will play Raccoons!" he announced loudly. Shane looked around. It meant Apple House would play whoever won the first round. The two teams lined up at each end of the rope.

"Look at Mark," Shane heard Peter say behind him.

Shane turned and looked. Mark was at the head of the team, joking with Serge, who was holding the rope right behind him.

It's weird, thought Shane. For someone who got so uptight in the downhill ski race, Mark seemed really laid-back. But when he sized up the two sides, Shane realized Crow House was definitely stronger. Sure, Raccoons had Keir Woodward, who was a good athlete, but that was a fluke. Almost from the day he arrived at Northwood, Shane had been told that Raccoon House was for the brains. Most of the kids in the house studied rather than played sports.

Quincy explained the rest of the rules, and started his countdown.

"One!"

The teams each picked up their ends of the rope and gripped it firmly. Mark and Keir headed the teams, each of them standing just behind one of the outside chalk lines.

"Two!"

The teams began to pull in opposite directions—just enough to pick up the slack left in the rope. The entire length rose into the air, with the red handkerchief in the middle bouncing above the center line. Mr. Rapoport ran forward and kneeled, eyeing the lineup between the handkerchief and the center blue line. When it looked right, he made a hand signal.

Boom!—the loud report of the Quince's starter pistol made everyone jump. It echoed back and forth between the mountains lining the valley, like thunder.

The contestants in the center of the field tensed. Mark Lepine roared like a caveman. The rope was totally taut, with every team member digging into the snow, and pulling back on the rope as hard as they could.

Shane watched the red handkerchief shift back and forth across the center line. First toward Crow House. Then, as the Raccoon team pulled harder it slowly wavered and went back across the line toward their side.

Mark roared again, and he was imitated by Serge, Sloan, and Renaldo. The Raccoon team's resistance melted, and the rope was pulled forward, tugging the handkerchief across Crow's blue line. The Raccoon team tumbled into each other and crashed into the snow. Everyone on the Crow team fell back on their behinds, laughing and slapping each other high-fives.

"Now we have to beat Crow House," Peter said quietly. He didn't sound very enthusiastic.

"And Mark Lepine," Shane added, remembering the unpleasant tantrum Mark had had when they hit the ice patch during the downhill ski race.

The Quince's amplified voice instructed the two remaining teams to take their places. "Apple House will now play Crow House, in the final match that will determine the winner of this year's Winter Murals, and the Quincy Cup!"

Shane looked at all the Apple House teammates. "Don't forget—when I yell 'Tug harder' you know what to do."

Everyone nodded solemnly. Across the second blue line, the Crow team was lining up along the rope. Mark Lepine eyed Apple House with a look of amused loathing.

Serge Williams jumped into line behind him. "We're going to flatten you guys," he yelled.

"Sure," Shane called out. "After we win the Tug-of-War, maybe."

"One!" The Quince's countdown started through the megaphone. The two teams lifted the rope, shifting into position.

"Two!"

Everyone stepped back one step, taking the remaining slack from the rope. The red handkerchief bobbed above the snow between them. Mr. Rapoport signaled.

Boom! Once again, like a clap of thunder, the report of the starting pistol ricocheted back and forth along the high Adirondack peaks guarding Northwood's valley.

Instantly, Shane felt the rope slipping in his hands. When he tried to grip it harder, it just pulled him forward. Ahead of him, the red handkerchief was sliding toward the Crow side.

"*Tug* the rope!" Shane cried. "*Tug* the rope!"

Instantly the whole team started shouting it, and with the first "*Tug!*", the rope began moving in their direction, pulling the handkerchief back almost to the center.

Cheers erupted from almost all students who were watching, while the kids from Moose House booed.

Mark Lepine gritted his teeth. He roared loudly.

Shane felt himself pulled slowly back toward the middle. He kept calling, *"Tug* the rope, *Tug* the rope!" this time even louder. His teammates followed his example, and pulled harder. Almost magically, when they were all tugging together, the rope began to move in their direction again.

Once again, Mark bellowed. *"Pulllll!"* he yelled at his teammates, realizing how the Apple House team used their cheer to pull at the same time. "Pull!" Mark yelled again.

The stocky boys from Crow House dug the heels of their boots into the snow, and began pulling in time to Mark's shouts. Shane, Lynn, Peter, Darlene, Delia, Corky, and Jeff felt the rope shifting, then pulling them forward.

"Tug the rope! *Tug* the rope!" they shouted together, but each time they applied their strength they lost ground to Crow House. Shane realized that despite all their efforts, Crow House was winning. There was only one thing left to do. He took a deep breath and yelled as loud as he could, *"Tug harder!"*

Then he opened his hands and let go of the rope.

CHAPTER 10

The Tug-of-War rope shot forward several inches, but instantly Shane grabbed it again, and gripped it fiercely. He tried to picture his fist as an iron vise. Down the line behind him, from Lynn to Peter, everyone did the same thing.

It was just enough to throw the Crow team off balance. Mark Lepine, Serge, Priscilla, and everyone jerked backward. The trick made the Crow team lose their footing. They started tripping over their own feet, then over each other.

"Tug the rope!" Shane shouted, before the Crow team realized what had happened. The Apple team pulled hard, throwing their last reserves of strength into the contest. Slowly at first, the rope began to tug in their direction.

"Tug the rope!" the Apple team cheered. *"Tug* the rope!"

They tugged the Crow team across the snow, until the

69

red handkerchief was well over the blue chalk line on their side.

It was over! There was a moment of silence, with only the cold cruel whistle of a strong wind blowing through the pine forest on the slopes of Mount Fear. Then the Quince's voice boomed across the field.

"The winner of this year's Winter Murals is Apple House!"

Shane felt a thrill of victory, and looked around at his teammates. His throat was raw from shouting so loud, and his arms ached. Everyone was panting hard, trying to catch their breath, but their eyes were sparkling with happiness. They had won!

Suddenly Shane heard an angry voice behind him. He spun around. Mark Lepine was marching angrily across the snow.

"You cheated!" he yelled. "You let go of the rope to throw us off balance."

"We didn't cheat," Lynn snapped. "We just used strategy. Remember strategy, Mark? I thought you knew all about it!"

"That . . . that . . . th—" Mark started stammering and his face was flushed red.

"It's not fair," Serge said loudly to no one in particular. "It's not fair."

"So what're you going to do about it, Lepine," Peter said aggressively. He walked between Shane and Mark and stood there, facing Mark down.

This is going too far, Mark thought. It was, after all, only a game, and not worth fighting about. "Come on,

Peter, it's just sour grapes,'' he said, putting his hand on Peter's shoulder and pulling him back.

"Yeah, Lepine's a sore loser," Jeff added, making Shane wince. Mark was backing off, but when he heard Jeff's comment, he started raising his fists.

Suddenly the Quince was standing among the kids with his hands on his hips, still clutching the megaphone with one hand. He looked annoyed, and his eyes flickered at Mark, then to the crowd of Northwood students.

"Mr. Lepine," Quincy said, addressing Mark formally the way he did when he was about to lay down the Northwood law. "Did you have a formal complaint to make about the Tug-of-War?" he demanded sternly.

Mark looked at Shane and Peter, his eyes still burning with fury. Then he turned around and faced the Quince. "No," he said. He forced himself to smile—quickly. "Apple won, fair and square." He muttered as if the words were stones in his mouth.

A chorus of boos began to rise from Moose House and the rest of the Crow team. "It's not fair," Serge said again, sounding like a broken record. The Quince signalled for silence.

"This is not the Northwood spirit," Lynn whispered quickly in Shane's ear. He was about to ask her what she meant when Quincy began to speak.

"This is not the Northwood spirit," he started. Lynn nudged Shane, and he realized this must be a pretty standard rap for the school's headmaster. The Quince continued. "The students from Apple House demonstrated two of our school's most enduring virtues—teamwork and strategy. They won a well-deserved victory here today. Now three cheers for Apple House, the winner of this year's Winter Murals!''

The whole school cheered with a lot more enthusiasm than there had been in the earlier booing. Only Serge, Priscilla, and a few of the kids in Moose House didn't cheer, Shane noticed. And he watched Mark turn and storm across the playing field toward Crow House without speaking to anyone.

When the cheers died down, Mr. Quincy announced that the make-your-own-sundae dinner was an hour away. The crowd of students drifted off to do their chores. Shane and Peter walked down toward the new barn to meet Tiny. With all this snow, Shane thought, maybe Tiny would let him drive the tractor again.

"You didn't have to jump in like that before, Peter,'' Shane said, remembering the standoff of a few minutes ago. "I can take care of myself. Especially against Mark Lepine.''

Peter smiled at him strangely. "Oh, it wasn't you I was worried about. I was afraid Mark would really persuade someone that we cheated. And I had six sundaes riding on it.''

"What?'' Shane exclaimed. "I thought you lost all your sundaes on the downhill ski race.''

"I did!'' Peter said happily. "All except my own. And I bet that six times.''

"Good thing we won—or you would have owed five different people sundaes tonight.''

Peter nodded. "Are you kidding?'' he said. "I'd be

lucky if I even left the dining hall alive. Staring down Mark Lepine was nothing compared to the trouble I'd be in if we'd lost.''

When Shane and Peter got to the new barn, Tiny was standing out front, bundled up in a bulky ski coat that made him look even more like Frankenstein. He was filling the gas tank in the tractor from the school's private tank.

''Shovels in the barn,'' the big, stoop-shouldered man said tersely, pointing to the building. ''You guys can start clearing the snow off Sky Walk.''

Shane felt crestfallen, and looked longingly at the tractor. As if reading his mind, Tiny grunted. ''I keep plowing the roads, but it's not doing any good. Too much snow.''

Shane and Peter saw the shovels as soon as they entered the barn. A portable radio was playing country music, but just as the two boys began to leave, the song was interrupted. An announcer warned of a blizzard alert in upstate New York.

''Come on,'' Shane said. ''We better tell Tiny.''

Tiny hardly reacted when he heard the news. ''Yup,'' he said matter-of-factly. ''I expect the road into the valley will be closed already. The snowdrifts are piling up and they don't wait for the sheriff's office to make it official.''

''You mean, Northwood's cut off?'' Shane asked.

'' 'Course it is,'' Peter said, and nudged him with his elbow. ''It usually happens once or twice a winter.''

''Haven't seen a blizzard like this in forty–fifty years,'' Tiny said, taking the gas nozzle from the tractor tank and hanging the hose up on the pump. ''Gonna be a bad one.''

Tiny must have seen the worry on their faces. " 'Course if there's an emergency," he assured them, "we can always bulldoze our way out with the tractor."

At dinner, Peter collected his debts—all the sundaes he'd won. He'd won a lot. In a burst of generosity, he lowered his wager. He just took a spoonful of each sundae—a humongous spoonful—so everyone got to eat most of their own dessert after all.

At the end of the meal, the Quince rose and walked to the front of the room. "And now last year's winner of the Quincy Cup will present it to this year's winners—Apple House!"

Mark Lepine appeared from the kitchen, still wearing his long white apron. He was beaming from ear to ear. High over his head for everyone to see he held the great Quincy Cup, an enormous silver bowl mounted on a rosewood base. Around the rim of the silver bowl, small brass crests were engraved with the names of each years' winners.

Mark good-naturedly shook their hands and passed on the Quincy Cup.

"Sorry I lost it this afternoon, Shane," Mark said. He laughed sheepishly. "I take sports real serious—maybe a little too serious sometimes."

Shane felt relieved. When they stopped shaking hands, Shane put out his hand for a high-five. "No problem, dude. You were a tough competitor."

Mark hand came down on Shane's with a loud clap, and the boys broke apart to the cheers of Northwood's student body.

CHAPTER 11

That night, the kids from Apple House returned home
with Peter and Shane carrying the Quincy Cup between
them, almost like a procession. For a year—until the next
Winter Murals—the Cup would reside over the fireplace
at Apple House.

Exhilarated from the day's events, everyone crowded
into the living room, still too excited to go to their rooms
for sleep. Jeff lit a fire in the hearth, and turned down the
lights. Soon the flames were roaring, their orange lights
dancing on the gleaming silver bowl of the Quincy Cup on
the mantel above.

"Hey, let's sing old Beatles songs," Darlene proposed.
She and Lynn had come back from Christmas break with
all their parents' old Beatles albums from the '60s. They'd
been listening to them over and over ever since.

"Great idea," Lynn seconded. Immediately the two
girls launched into a boisterous off-key version of
"Norwegian Wood." When they were finished, Kevin

jumped in front of the fireplace, playing the air guitar, and screaming out the words to "Twist and Shout." Soon everyone—even Mr. and Mrs. Durrell, who knew all the words—joined in.

After that, Jeff did his Freddy Mercury imitation using a long broomstick for a pretend guitar. With the song playing loudly, he strummed on the broom's whisks and lyp-synched to "We Are the Champions." By the time he was finished, everyone was doubled over with laughter. Mrs. Durrell came in carrying a huge tray of late-night steaming hot toddies—mulled apple cider.

Only Shane sat away from the rest of the kids, his head still filled with thoughts of the day's events. He was disturbed by the strange sabotage of the Winter Murals, and couldn't stop thinking about it. He remembered the cut rope on the toboggan, and the rocks on the cross-country ski trail. It had all been forgotten in the jubilation that followed Apple House's Tug-of-War victory. But Shane was sure that whoever had done it—Grat or someone else—wanted to hurt Northwood's students. What if Grat was still out there, just waiting for the right moment to attack someone?

The fire roaring in the hearth heated the room, but Shane felt himself shiver. Mrs. Durrell handed him a cup of hot apple cider. As soon as Shane started sipping at the spiced drink, he began to feel drowsy. He was acutely aware that his hands were still sore from the Tug-of-War contest. Some of his muscles ached, too—especially where he'd fallen on the icy slope in the wipeout with Mark Lepine.

The living room was quiet. Although it was still fairly early, everyone else also seemed to have become aware of just how tired they really were. Barely able to keep his eyes open, Shane announced he was going up to bed. His decision was seconded around the room, and soon most of the kids were heading upstairs.

Shane brushed his teeth and walked into the bedroom, where Peter was already turning down his own bed.

"So do you really think old man Grat is out to get us?" Shane asked in a solemn tone. "I mean, with the rope on the toboggan being cut, and the rocks piled on the ski trail?"

Peter shrugged without even glancing at him. "Definitely it was a Grat attack," he said, hopping into bed and pulling the blankets up. "He's got motive—revenge against the Quincy family—and he's crazy. What more do you need to know?" Peter leaned over to click off the bedside lamp, and fell back in his bed, curled on his side with his eyes closed.

Shane got into bed. The north wind outside rattled the glass in the window frames and howled around the eaves. He fell asleep quickly, and woke with a start sometime later. Peter was standing near the door, fully dressed and pulling on his parka. It was almost midnight on the clock radio.

Shane sat up. "Where are you going?"

Peter was startled. He swung around and put his finger to his lips. "I'm going for my stash. You want me to bring you back a chocolate bar? I have some extras."

"You're going out in that?" Shane asked incredulously. Outside, the north wind roared, and snow blowing against the window sounded like pins thrown on glass. It was falling so thickly, it was impossible to see more than fifteen or twenty feet beyond the house.

Peter grinned at him. "Sure. No one else will be out there, so I don't have to worry about anyone finding out where I keep it."

He grasped the door handle, opened it, and slipped into the hall. Shane sank back on his pillow and watched the thin line of light from the corridor narrow and blink out. He was still groggy and closed his eyes for sleep. Suddenly, the image of old man Grat, ranting and raving in the doorway of the dining hall, popped into his head. *What if Grat's out there now?* Shane wondered. Peter might be in danger.

Shane's eyes opened and he stared at the ceiling, debating whether to be concerned—or to go back to the land of dreams that his tired body longed for. Peter was his friend. Shane realized there was no way he could just let him go out into the storm alone—not if there was danger there.

Shane threw back the covers, and swung out of bed. He dressed quickly and left the room. In the hall, he ran into Lynn wearing her bathrobe. She looked at Shane strangely. "You going out into *that?*"

"Uh, yeah. Peter just went for his stash," he told her quietly. "After that stuff that happened today, I suddenly got paranoid about him being out there alone. You know, in case of a Grat attack or whatever."

"Wait for me," Lynn told him. "I'll get dressed and come with you. Give me two minutes, okay?"

When they stepped outside, gusts of wind drove hard tiny flakes of snow into their faces and almost blew them off the steps. There was no sign of Peter.

"You have any idea where he keeps it?" Shane asked. He almost had to shout to be heard over the howling wind.

Lynn pointed toward Mount Lookout. "He told me it's somewhere up near the toboggan shed," she said. "But he never showed me exactly where."

They started walking down Sky Walk, bending their bodies forward against the power of the cold wind. The snow was piled in slowly changing drifts. The path that Shane and Peter had cleared only a few hours earlier was already obliterated.

When they reached the road that led past the barn to the slopes of Mount Lookout, Shane heard Lynn gasp behind him. He swung around, and saw her looking at Mount Fear, almost invisible behind the thick curtain of snow.

"What's the matter?" Shane demanded.

Lynn turned around, looked at him, and just shook her head, as if to say "nothing." She started to walk past him, but Shane stopped her.

"What?" Shane asked more firmly.

"Nothing!" Lynn said loudly. She was about to walk on when she hesitated and bit her lip. Then she looked at Shane again. "I thought I saw lights blinking through the snowstorm. Up on Mount Fear."

Shane turned and gazed toward the mountain. He couldn't see anything.

"It's gone now," Lynn said. "But I was sure I saw a flashing light up there!"

Shane sighed. "Someone's up there with a flashlight or a lantern," he said, looking at Lynn. "I mean, that's the only possible explanation—unless you believe in ghosts. And I don't."

Reluctantly, Lynn nodded and tore her gaze away from the mountain. "I guess so," she said in a hesitant voice. "It's just that . . . well, it's dangerous up there on that ledge. Who would go up there to shine lights in a storm like this?"

Lynn turned and started in the direction Peter had gone. Shane waited a moment, staring through the blowing snow at the terrible peak. He could see absolutely nothing, except the great dark shape of the mountain rising over the forest. Definitely no lights. *Is everyone around here going crazy?* he thought. He turned around, and followed Lynn.

CHAPTER 12

Kneeling down near the foundation of the toboggan shed, Peter reached into his secret stash hole. When his hand pulled back, it was full of candy bars. Peter's stomach had been rumbling ominously ever since dinner, and his favorite prescription for a stomachache was to eat more. He carefully pushed the rock back into place to hide the hole. The snow will cover my tracks by morning, he thought. No one will ever know.

Suddenly, he thought he heard his name called. He froze, a chill of fear climbing up his spine and clutching the base of his skull. He felt hair on the back of his neck prickle.

"Who's there?" he demanded, jumping to his feet. He strained his ears to listen. Finally, he heard it again. It was a low, eerie howl behind him, mingling with the sound of the wind.

"Oooooooooooo . . . Peeeeterrrrr . . . commmmme to me . . . !"

He spun around, jumping almost three feet in the air. His eyes were the size of saucers. His mouth made a round circle of terror. Candy bars flew in all directions, and Peter tumbled back into the snow.

Shane and Lynn burst into view from behind some trees, laughing hysterically. Peter eyed them angrily from his seat in the snow. The drift he'd fallen into was higher than his shoulders. He didn't look as if he appreciated the joke.

"You guys!" Peter said, almost angrily. "What are you doing, spying on me so you can raid my stash?"

"Sure, that's why we came out of hiding," Shane said sarcastically.

"We were worried about you," Lynn told him. "We thought old man Grat might be wandering around trying to kill a Northwood student or something."

Shane put out his hand and helped Peter to his feet.

"Really?" Peter asked, still a little doubtful.

"Really," Shane assured him, nodding for emphasis.

"Well," Peter grumbled, looking around at the snow in an effort to spot the candy. "I'd offer you a chocolate bar but—"

"Here's one," Lynn said, plucking a package from a small hole in the snow. "And there's another." She pointed to Peter's side, where a yellow wrapper poked out of the snow that nearly covered it.

In almost no time they'd found four chocolate bars. After a few more minutes of looking, they gave up on the fifth one. Peter gave them each a Snickers bar. "That still leaves one for me and one that I can barter," he said, relieved.

They started back to Apple House, pulling their scarves up against the biting wind. It howled at their backs and urged them forward, almost as if coaxing them to hurry. They had nearly reached the barns when Shane stopped Lynn and Peter with a raised hand.

"I saw someone over there!" he said quickly. "And I'm positive he was wearing a red jacket!"

"Another Grat attack!" Peter exclaimed.

"Maybe this time we really should tell the Quince," Lynn suggested cautiously.

Shane thought a moment, staring through the falling snow. The area in front of the barns was lit by bright outdoor lights over each of the great doors. The person he'd seen had been walking in snowshoes across the open space. Now he'd darted into the woods on the other side.

"What should we do?" Peter asked.

"Let's look at the footprints before they get snowed over," Shane proposed. "So we can give the Quince as much information as possible."

They found the trail of snowshoe prints leading from the door of the new barn and around the side.

"To me, they look the same as the tracks we saw last night," Lynn announced. Shane and Peter nodded their agreement.

"But what was Grat doing in the barn?" Peter asked in an ominous tone.

"We don't know for sure it *was* Grat," Shane pointed out. He started following the prints around the corner of the barn. They were rapidly being covered by blowing snow, but he could see them leading straight into the woods. "Let's see where they go," he proposed.

They followed the snowshoe tracks, lifting their legs high to get through the thick snowdrifts in the forest. More than once, they found themselves sinking up to their waists. Soon though, they were standing beside an ancient, crumbling fence. Made of old logs, it zigzagged crazily along a field. It must once have been used for farming, but now the field was slowly returning to woodland, thanks to years of neglect. The trail led across the field and disappeared near a copse of small trees. Beyond it, almost invisible in the driving snow, Shane made out the outline of a big old house. A dim, yellow light burned in a single window.

"Spooky," he said softly.

"Haven't you ever seen Grat's house?" Peter asked.

Shane shook his head.

"It's a total disaster," Peter said. He still wasn't feeling very well. The rumbling in his stomach seemed to be getting worse. Still, it wouldn't take more than a minute to show Shane the crumbling old farmhouse. And it made Peter feel important to be able to show off his inside knowledge to the new kid. "I'll show it to you," he offered eagerly. "Let's get closer."

"No, we shouldn't," Lynn warned quickly. "It's against the rules—and you know how old man Grat gets if he thinks someone from Northwood's been on his land."

"So?" Peter retorted. "In minutes in this snow our footprints will be completely drifted over. No one will

84

ever know." Peter leaped across the rickety fence with surprising agility for a boy his size. The rumbling in his stomach was forgotten in his excitement. He started toward the trees where the footprints disappeared.

Shane looked at Lynn, and saw her alarm. "Just to see the house?" he asked. "After all, we've come this far."

"I guess," Lynn said slowly.

A few minutes later they crouched low in a snowdrift, looking across the snow-covered side yard at the house fifty feet away. A square of yellow light glowed across the snow from the window, and Shane could see weedy tufts of dead grass sticking up through the snowdrifts covering the yard. The lawn underneath hadn't been cut in a long time.

The hulking, two-story colonial house was equally neglected. The wood sides were weathered and gray from lack of paint. Its windowsills were crumbling, and tilted off kilter. Shingles seemed to be missing from large patches of the roof. A porch at the back had completely collapsed against the main house. Ragged curtains seemed to cover most of the windows, except the room where the light burned. Still, it was impossible to see inside, because the panes of glass were so filthy.

"I want to see in that window," Peter hissed.

"No, Peter!" Lynn said in an angry whisper. "This is *not* a good idea. I mean it."

It was too late. Peter had broken away from them, and was already sneaking closer and closer to the house.

"Peter! Come back!" Shane tried to call quietly. The wind howled as he spoke, tossing the gaunt, bare branches of the shrub beside them. "Wait here," he told Lynn. "I'll go get him!"

"I'm not staying here by myself."

They left their cover, and followed Peter toward the house. Peter was only a few feet from the porch, and Lynn and Shane were twenty feet behind him. Suddenly, the front door flew open. Shane and Lynn froze. Cornelius Grat's enormous hulk was outlined by the light in the room behind him. His massive hair and beard glowed around the edges like fire.

"Who's there?" the crazy old man hollered over the sounds of the storm. "Spying on me, are you!" Immediately he spotted Peter, standing knee-deep in snow barely ten feet away. "Thief! Come to steal again?"

Grat's arms moved swiftly, and an enormous axe appeared in them. He swung it over his head, the sharp blade glinting in the light from the house, and ran toward them.

"I'm going to chop you up!" the lunatic neighbor screamed. "I'll teach you to steal, you rotten thief! I'm going to chop you into little, tiny pieces!"

CHAPTER 13

"Into the woods!" Shane shouted. He grabbed Lynn's hand and started running through the deep snow, with Peter behind them.

"Thieves! Thieves! I'll teach you to spy and steal!" Grat howled again. This time, his terrible voice competed with the howling wind. Shane glanced back. The old man was floundering in knee-deep snowdrifts and falling behind.

"I'll cut off your heads, thieves!"

"Hurry, Peter!" Shane yelled.

"I am!" Peter shouted back. He was running frantically to get as far as possible from old man Grat. He felt like his lungs were going to pop. He could hear the enormous axe swooshing back and forth behind him through the empty air.

Shane and Lynn reached the edge of the forest and clung to a tree, panting heavily. Peter was closing in on them. Further back in the middle of the overgrown field, almost up to his hips in snow, old man Grat swung the axe through the air so hard it threw him off balance.

"I'll teach you to steal my—" He tumbled sideways, following the weight of the steel head, and went down in a deep drift just as Peter reached the woods.

"Come on!" Shane hissed anxiously, grabbing Peter's hand and pulling him into the woods.

"Stop, thieves—" Grat's voice rumbled behind them, growing fainter as they went deeper and deeper into the woods. Gaunt black tree trunks stuck up from a flat endless plain of snow that sparkled dully in the strange gray light. Finally, they were far enough that Grat's screams could no longer reach them. The north wind swept along the cold, naked branches of the trees overhead, ferociously driving snow against them.

Shane and Lynn went in front to clear a path through the deep snow for Peter, who was less athletic. After several minutes of silent hiking through the knee-high snow, they found their original tracks. They began to retrace them back to Northwood, on the snow-covered path through the forest.

"Wait up," Peter called breathlessly, still stumbling through the woods.

"Just hurry!" Lynn snapped. "We should never have gone onto Grat's land. And when we get back to Northwood we're telling the Quince everything."

"I'm not feeling very well," he pleaded weakly, his voice lost among the dark tree trunks and the night.

Lynn spun around while Shane trudged on through the snow. She saw Peter's dark form lurching from tree to tree. "You said you were sick a while ago, too, but it didn't stop you from trespassing on Grat's land and almost getting us killed!''

Ahead of them on the trail, Shane stopped and looked back. ''You're just upset because you're scared, Peter. It was totally chilling.''

Lynn waited on the trail. ''You know, we could get expelled—'' She broke off when Peter stumbled from the trees and wobbled onto the open trail. In the eerie moonlight his face glowed a sickening shade of green.

Peter looked at Lynn, shaking his head, slowly. ''No, I feel real sick. I feel like I'm going to—''

Before he could finish the sentence, Peter doubled over and dropped to his knees. Then he was sick in the snow.

Lynn ran to him. ''Shane,'' she called, kneeling beside Peter. ''He really is sick!''

Shane stomped back until he found Peter and Lynn huddled in the middle of the trail. Peter was shivering violently, and Shane knew it wasn't just from the cold.

''All those chocolate fudge sundaes you ate . . .'' Shane began.

Peter shook his head. ''It feels worse than that,'' he said weakly.

''Maybe it's the flu,'' Lynn suggested.

Shane knelt and put his arm under Peter's. ''Come on, Lynn and I will help you back,'' he said, helping him to stand up. He motioned down the trail. ''It's only a few hundred feet. Just along the trail and downhill to the barns.''

They staggered through the deep snow, with Lynn and Shane on each side and Peter in middle. Icy blasts of cold, snowy wind almost knocked them back. Frost began to nip their noses and ears. Even their fingers in their gloves and their toes inside their boots began to feel the icy sting.

Shane saw a slight glow of light, almost like a halo rising above the snow ahead, highlighting the steadily falling flakes that descended from the night sky, like stars falling to earth. It was the lights of Northwood. But he was little prepared for the sight that met their eyes when they turned the corner.

Up and down the valley, beaming through the trees and across the great lawns of Northwood, every single window in every house was blazing with light.

"The whole school is up!" Shane exclaimed.

"Gosh, I hope they're not looking for us," Lynn moaned, sure that they were going to be in even worse trouble.

Shane sighed and looked at Lynn. "I guess we'll find out soon enough."

Standing between them, and holding on for dear life, Peter groaned. "Can you guys help me to the nurse's office?" he mumbled faintly.

"Sure we will, dude," Shane told him. "Everything's gonna be fine."

They started down the path to the small, shingled cabin near the dining hall where Mrs. Rhinebeck, the nurse, lived. As they approached, they could hear doors slamming, and muffled shouts through the windy air. When the dining hall came into view, they saw a stream of kids and some of the counselors and teachers going inside, moving slowly, with some people holding up others.

Through the brightly lit windows it was apparent that the dining hall was crowded. The newly fallen snow had been packed down in all directions from foot traffic.

"Something's going on," Shane said out loud, voicing Lynn's thoughts. Peter hardly seemed to be conscious. He sagged between them, and would have fallen if they hadn't held him up. They pushed forward, almost dragging the sick boy until they were near the front steps. As they approached, the Quince walked out the front doors. His face looked white and worried, and he was moving slowly, as if he were in pain.

"Mr. Quincy!" Lynn and Shane called together.

The headmaster looked up and when he saw them he seemed enormously relieved. "Thank goodness, there you are," he said, almost groaning.

"Peter's sick," Lynn said quickly. "He threw up in the woods and can barely walk." As she spoke, they helped Peter up the steps.

"Get him inside where it's warm," the Quince instructed, opening the door. He winced, and put his hand to his stomach. "Everyone's sick. All the students. The teachers. The nurse, even Tiny, everyone."

Shane and Lynn helped Peter through the door, and for the first time they saw how serious the problem was. There were at least thirty or forty kids there, wrapped in blankets and sitting at the tables or lying on the floor. Nurse Rhinebeck moved slowly among them, feeling foreheads and checking thermometers. Miss Pebbels hovered nearby, pouring glasses of water for students. She looked white and sickly herself.

Shane and Lynn's eyes met with a questioning look. "Are you sick?" Shane asked her, as they helped Peter slowly to a bench at the nearest table.

Lynn shook her head. "Uh-uh."

The Quince looked at them sharply. "You're not?" He eased himself down onto a bench and looked up at them, one hand still clutching his stomach, and his mouth grimacing with pain. "What did you eat tonight?" he demanded.

Lynn and Shane looked puzzled. They heard a loud thump. When they turned around they saw Peter collapsed unconscious on the dining hall floor!

CHAPTER 14

"He's out cold!" Shane said. Immediately he knelt by Peter's side, loosening his collar. Lynn rolled up his jacket and pushed it under his head.

Mrs. Rhinebeck came over and knelt by the unconscious boy, feeling his forehead with the flat of her hand and then taking his pulse. "There's only one thing that could make everyone this sick so quickly," she said grimly. "Food poisoning."

"That's what I was getting at," Mr. Quincy said to Shane and Lynn. "It had to be something everyone ate—except you two."

Shane looked at Lynn. "What *didn't* we eat?" Almost immediately it connected. "Ice cream! I'm allergic to dairy so I didn't have any for dessert tonight."

"But I had some," Lynn pointed out. Then her eyes grew big. "But I didn't have any chocolate fudge sauce! Neither of us did!"

Mr. Quincy nodded weakly. "That must have been it.

Somehow it must have been contaminated with something.''

"We need to get this boy to a hospital," Mrs. Rhinebeck said, her voice filled with alarm. She was kneeling beside Peter, stroking his hair. His face was white, and his breathing came in short raspy breaths. "He's as cold as ice. I think he's going into a coma. If we don't get medical help, he might die!''

"Right," Lynn said slowly. "Peter ate more than anyone.''

"All those desserts he won," Shane finished.

"We need help," Nurse Rhinebeck said. "Peter needs urgent medical care—more than I can give him here, although I'll do my best.''

"The telephones are down," the Quince explained. "And the roads are impassable.''

The Quince looked at Shane. His eyes were filled with pain, and he gripped his stomach. Then he fought against it to speak in a calm, steady voice. "You help Tiny out, don't you? Didn't I see you on the tractor this morning?''

"Yes, sir," Shane said quickly. "He lets me plow the snow out around the barns, and pick up the mail sometimes.''

"Do you think you can drive it down to the main road?'' Quincy asked.

Shane thought carefully for a moment. With its enormous tires, and the blade on the front, snowdrifts were no problem. And the closed cab would protect him from the wind and driving snow. Still, he'd never driven anything—let alone a tractor—all by himself. But there was no one else to do it.

He nodded. "Sure. At least, I'm pretty sure."

Quince nodded, his lips tight, forcing back the pain. "Good lad. It's a dangerous assignment, but you've got to get help."

"I'll go with him, sir," Lynn said, stepping forward and standing in front of the Quince. The headmaster looked at her, almost taken aback. "In case something happens, sir. It'd be better if there were two of us."

Quince looked at them and nodded weakly. "Yes, of course. Hurry, but be very careful. And good luck."

Shane and Lynn left the dining hall. As soon as they were outside, Shane said, "I always thought food poisoning only came from things like meat and fish and eggs."

Lynn nodded. "Me, too. Unless . . ." She met Shane's eyes and they both knew what the other was thinking. "Unless someone . . ."

"Put something in the chocolate fudge sauce to poison the entire school," Shane finished for her. "Just like someone cut the rope on the toboggan and piled the rocks on the ski trail."

"Someone like Grat," Lynn said softly.

Shane looked puzzled. "But how could old man Grat put poison in the chocolate fudge sauce?"

Lynn shrugged. "He came right into the dining hall the night before last at dinner. He could have snuck in when no one was looking."

Shane nodded slowly, not entirely convinced. "Yeah, I guess."

They reached Apple House, where Mr. and Mrs. Durrell were waiting for them, white and tight-lipped. "Everyone here is sick, too," they told Shane and Lynn when they heard what was happening in the dining hall.

Shane and Lynn each added several more layers of T-shirts and sweaters under their coats. At Jeff's suggestion—made in a grim voice when he emerged from the bathroom—they both doubled the socks they wore, with thin plastic bags between one of the layers. They rolled the tops of their socks up over their jeans, and tied their hiking boots tightly right up to the top hole.

Mrs. Durrell insisted that they each take an extra scarf, too. By the time they finished dressing, with their wool ski hats and scarves, little was visible except their eyes.

They left Apple House and raced toward the barn where the tractor was parked. The blizzard seemed to have ebbed slightly. The air was still thick with heavy flakes and icy cold, but the fury of the wind was gone. Shane and Lynn pulled open the barn's big double doors, kicking away the snow that blocked them. Bare light-bulbs strung down the center beams illuminated the inside. The tractor was parked in the center.

Shane swallowed. For some reason, it looked a lot bigger than it had a few days earlier, when he'd last driven it. It looked enormous, especially with the huge snow blade on the front. The rear tires alone were as tall as he was.

"I'll get it started." He climbed up into the seat. When he was a kid, his dad used to take him go-cart racing at a local track, and he'd learned how to shift gears. But a tractor had five gears—not three like a little go-cart. And it was more like riding an elephant instead of a pony.

Shane pulled out the choke, turned the key, and pressed the ignition button. The engine started, almost caught—and then stalled. He pressed the ignition again and the same thing happened. He tried a third time. The starter strained over and over, and Shane tried feeding it more gas. This time the engine didn't start at all.

Shane looked down from the cab at Lynn. "I'm sure I'm doing everything right," he said, puzzled. "It sounds like it isn't getting any gas." He looked over the dashboard and decided to try starting it with the choke closed. But again, the engine refused to start.

"Shane!" Lynn called to him from behind the tractor.

Shane leaned forward in his seat and stuck his head out the window of the little cab. He saw her standing near the rear wheel and she held a gas cap up for him to see.

"This was lying on the ground," she told him. "And there's white stuff all over the fender where you fill the tank."

Shane jumped down from the cab. It looked as if someone had spilled fine white sand over the polished green fender. Shane licked his finger, picked up a few grains, and sniffed them.

"Look at this!" Lynn said. She was peering under the huge tires. She reached in a hand and pulled out a crumpled white and blue package. "An empty bag of sugar."

Shane looked at the tiny white crystals on his finger. It looked like sugar to him. He tasted them. "Definitely sugar!" he exclaimed. He opened the metal door that covered the hole for the gas tank. More of the white crystals spilled down over the fender. The inside of the little compartment was filled with it. "Someone's poured sugar in the gas tank!"

Lynn looked puzzled. "Is that why it doesn't start?"

"You bet it is," Shane said. "It's totally clogged everything up. And someone did this deliberately—just like he poisoned the chocolate fudge sauce."

Lynn felt a chill of fear tingling at the base of her spine. "Now there's no way out! No way to get help!"

"Shane! Lynn!"

They heard their names called and turned just in time to see Mark materialize through the falling snow at the open doors of the barn.

"The Quince told me you guys were out here," he said when he spotted them beside the tractor. "I skipped the chocolate fudge sundaes, too," he added, approaching them. "Uh, you know, because of my special diet and all. I came to see if you need some help."

Shane and Lynn quickly told Mark everything—their sightings of someone in a red jacket lurking in the woods, their suspicions that the Winter Murals had been sabotaged, their grim escape from Grat's land.

Mark listened, his eyes growing wider. "No way," he said, finally. "You've been hanging with Peter too much, and now you're believing in ghosts, too."

"Oh yeah?" Shane asked. "And did a ghost do this?" He held up the empty sugar bag and pointed to the sugar around the tractor's gas tank.

Mark seemed really shocked. Then he nodded slowly.

"Maybe Grat's behind it after all," he said. "Whoever it is, the whole school is sick, and cut off from help."

"There's got to be some way of getting help," Lynn pleaded.

Shane nodded. "Everyone's really sick. Especially Peter. The nurse said he could even die. We've got to do something."

Mark looked at them. "I know I was a little rough on you guys today during the Murals, but I'm willing to help however I can. For the Northwood spirit—teamsmanship and strategy. But the only way out of the valley now is across—"

"I know," Shane nodded. "We have to climb Mount Fear."

CHAPTER 15

"B-but, it's not possible," Lynn stammered.

"Sure it is," Mark said. "Benjamin Quincy and Martin Grat did it to warn the American army about the British."

"But Martin Grat didn't make it," Lynn pointed out. "And in this blizzard, it would be suicide."

"Actually, the dangerous part of the ledge is only about ten feet long," Mark told them. "It's easy once you're on the other side . . ."

"How do you know?" Lynn asked sharply.

"All the kids at Northwood—except new kids—have hiked up there," Mark replied. "You have, too."

"Sure," Lynn acknowledged. "But only on class hikes. And no one's allowed to go across the ledge to the other side."

Mark looked embarrassed. "Last Halloween I went up there with Keith and Renaldo to scare Peter and Serge."

"That was you!" Lynn exclaimed.

Mark gave a little laugh. "Yeah, Serge told me what he

100

and Peter were doing—dangling lights off the ledge to scare people. So we snuck up ahead of them, and hid in the bushes. You should have seen the looks on their faces when we jumped out. I've never seen Peter or Serge run so fast!''

Mark continued. ''Don't tell the Quince, but afterward we hammered spikes—pitons, actually—into the rock and strung a rope from one side to the other. Then we hung onto the rope and went across. It was easy.''

Mark looked around the barn and saw the heavy tug-of-war rope slung over the side of an empty stall. He tugged it down and hung it across his shoulder. ''We have the rope. And I'm sure the spikes are still in the rock.'' When Shane and Lynn remained silent, Mark said in frustration, ''How else are we going to save Peter and everyone else?''

Shane turned to Lynn. ''We should do it,'' he said. ''At least it's worth trying.''

Lynn thought a moment longer. Finally, she nodded.

''I'll run over to the dining hall and tell the Quince what we're doing,'' Mark volunteered. ''I'll be back in five.''

Without waiting for an answer, he slipped out into the falling snow. Shane closed the doors to keep the wind and snow out, and they waited. A few minutes later, one of the double doors opened, and Mark slipped inside. He had a nylon knapsack over his shoulders.

''It's a go from the Quince as long as we use the rope!'' he called to them. ''He says the whole school's relying on us.''

Shane picked up the long coil of rope and they plunged out into the cold, snowy night.

They picked up the trail to Mount Fear behind the old barn, and entered the woods that blanketed the gentle, lower slopes. Although the trail was wide and smooth, it was a continuous uphill walk through deep snow. Soon, the three of them were huffing and puffing.

Shane had never been into this part of the valley. He didn't know if it was because of the night or the weird circumstances that put him there in the middle of a blizzard, but the forest seemed different here. The trees all looked more ancient, gnarled and twisted like something in a horror movie. There were no evergreens on Mount Fear, and all the maples had long since lost their leaves. With their rambling bare branches reaching skyward, it seemed to some as if he were walking through a dead world. The snow seemed to glow in the moonlight, giving off a pale and ghastly luminescence that grew shapes in the storm.

Overhead, Shane noticed that the north wind howled steadily, tossing branches and crashing them against each other with dull booms that sounded like distant thunder. Shane stopped to catch his breath. The great dark mass of Mount Fear loomed overhead like a jagged tooth.

Suddenly, he saw the dull glow of a light blinking on and off on the narrow ledge that led across the mountain to the other side. He felt a violent shiver ripple up his spine, and he knew it wasn't from the freezing cold. Was someone up there? Or was it truly the ghost lights of Mount Fear, the spirit of Martin Grat haunting the steep mountain pass where he had fallen to his death two hundred years earlier?

"Lynn! Mark!" Shane shouted loudly over the rising howl of the blizzard. The two others had staggered ahead of him and didn't hear. Shane pushed on until he was at their side.

"Did you see anything up on the ledge?" he demanded. Mark looked at him, perplexed.

"What?" Lynn shouted back. As they had climbed higher the wind had grown stronger. Shane needed to shout to be heard over its howling.

"Lights!" Shane yelled. "I saw lights up there."

Lynn pressed her lips together without answering, and looked at Mark, who shrugged and shook his head.

"It must be some kind of reflection," Mark assured him. He turned and started back up the mountain. "Come on, we have to hurry!"

Shane gritted his teeth and kept following. The forest dwindled, and the trail opened up on a snow-swept plateau strewn with enormous boulders. They were right under the mountaintop, which rose several hundred feet above them, dark and foreboding. On their left, the plateau ended abruptly at a sheer vertical face of craggy rock forty feet high.

"That's the ledge we have to cross over there," Mark shouted to Lynn and Shane, pointing near the base of the high rock face.

Shane shucked off the thick coil of rope. He could barely make out a thin, darker line at the base of the cliff. A dozen feet on the other side of it, the ground opened up into another wide plateau. From there it was straight downhill to the town of Peace Lake.

"I'll go find the pitons," Mark told them. He started walking toward the ledge.

Shane thought he heard another sound competing with the wind. He looked up and saw something dark and thin flying through the air overhead.

"What's—"

He broke off as he felt a something slipping down over his head.

"Hey!" Lynn yelled.

It was a loop of rope like a lasso, Shane realized. Before he could move, he felt it tighten around him and Lynn, pinning their arms to their sides. The end of the rope led across the snow to a dark cleft between two rocks. It was pulled taut, tugging them both toward the rock. Mark stood still nearby, staring in fear and amazement.

"Mark, help us!" Shane shouted.

Instead of coming to their rescue, Mark backed away several feet. Shane and Lynn felt the rope tugging them relentlessly toward the rocks.

"Mark!" Lynn called, her voice rising with panic.

Without saying a word, Mark turned tail and ran through the snow toward the safety of the treeline. Once again, the rope around them tightened, almost pulling Lynn and Shane to their knees.

Shane dug his boots into the snow and tried to resist. "Pull back!" he told Lynn. "Tug the rope!"

Although their upper arms were pinned to their sides, they both had their hands free. They wriggled their hands up enough and gripped the rope as best they could. They started tugging.

"*Tug* the rope, *tug* the rope!" Shane shouted rhythmically, imitating the chant that had helped Apple House win the Tug-of-War contest in the Winter Murals. It was no use. Shane and Lynn found themselves being steadily pulled, bit by bit, toward the rocks. As they came closer, Shane noticed a dim, yellowish glow coming from the crack.

"Let's give it some slack," Shane suggested. "Just like we did in the Murals today."

Lynn nodded. They both took several quick steps in the direction they were being pulled. For a moment the rope went slack.

"Now pull!" Shane yelled.

They both tightened their grip and tried to back up. Instead, the rope went taut again, and pulled them closer to the narrow opening in the rocks. This time, when they really needed it, their tug-of-war strategy wasn't working. Instead, the rope pulled them harder and harder, threatening to pull them down and drag them across the snow when they resisted.

Then they heard the terrible voice from the cleft in the rocks. It was a voice both of them had been dreading— and half-expecting.

"I've got you now, thieves!" Cornelius Grat thundered.

CHAPTER 16

The rope jerked hard. Shane and Lynn tumbled into the snow, their arms and legs totally tangled. Still they were being dragged relentlessly through the snow. As they came closer and closer to the rock, the dull, yellow glow grew brighter and brighter.

Suddenly, they were lying at the low entrance of a cave in the rocks. Shane saw an enormous bulky figure crouching in the opening.

"Now I have you, little thieves!" Cornelius Grat sneered. "I'll teach you to steal from me!" He grabbed them roughly by their jacket collars and dragged them into the cave.

With his arms still pinned tightly to his sides by the lasso, Shane raised his head and looked around. It was sheltered from the wind, and almost warm in the cave, which was dry and free of snow. It looked as if Grat had been camping there. An old canvas cot was covered with dirty blankets. Nearby a row of kerosene lanterns flickered.

Shane looked up at the shambling old man who towered above him. "It was you all along, wasn't it?" Shane said angrily. "There's no ghost up here—just you swinging those lanterns so people would think there was."

A strange laugh rumbled from Grat's throat. He seemed to smile at Shane and Lynn. His eyes glowed with an insane glint.

"You think you're mighty clever, you and that Quincy, don't you? Sending you over to rob me, to steal my clothes and my snowshoes. But I've got you now!"

"I don't know what you're talking about," Shane said. "We haven't stolen anything." He struggled against the rope, but it was pulled too tight. With Grat standing right over them, there was no way they could escape.

"You can't fool me anymore," Grat said. "I'm going to tie you up and take you to the sheriff. For two hundred years, the Quincy family has been stealing and trespassing on Grat land. Now I'll put a stop to the Quincy shenanigans once and for all."

"Oh yeah?"

Shane looked over to the entrance of the cave and saw Mark standing in the opening.

"You!" Grat shouted, almost as if he recognized the boy.

Mark rushed Grat with his hands out, pushing the old man back. Grat lost his balance, and felt back on the floor.

"Quick! Untie yourselves!" Mark shouted to Shane and Lynn. Grat started to rise, but Mark pushed him again. Once more, the old man stumbled to his knees.

Frantically, Shane felt around the rope that encircled them until his fingers found the slip knot. He started pulling at it. The rope began to slide through the loop. A second later, it was loose. He flung it over his head, and pulled Lynn out of the lasso.

Grat stood, a great lumbering giant, and took a step toward Mark. "I know your face. You're the one, the thief who stole my—" He leaped for Mark, who barely dodged him. Grat bellowed angrily, and turned to give chase.

Shane and Lynn struggled to their feet. Now it was three against one.

"Get him!" Lynn shouted.

The three Northwood students rushed the old man simultaneously, pushing him out of the cave. Seeing himself outnumbered, the old man's eyes were suddenly wide with terror. He opened his mouth and let out a blood-curdling scream of rage and fury.

Then he turned and fled outside into the blizzard.

Once he was gone, an eerie silence and the sound of their own heavy breathing filled the cave. Outside, the winds still howled fiercely. Lynn was the first to speak.

"What was all that about?" she wondered. "He kept calling us thieves and said he would teach us not to steal from him."

Mark shrugged. "Who knows? Grat's obviously crazy. Maybe after this, they'll commit him."

Shane looked at Mark with a warm smile. "I thought you chickened out back there when you took off. I guess I owe you an apology for that."

"And a big thanks for coming to our rescue," Lynn added.

Mark shrugged modestly. "When that lasso came down around you two, I didn't know what was happening. I figured I should lay low a few minutes until I knew.

"A lot of really sick people are counting on us to get through to Peace Lake," Mark continued. "And we don't have much further to go."

"Yeah, just the hard part," Lynn said. "Across the ledge."

Mark ducked out of the cave and came back with his knapsack and the coil of rope. He took out three strong leather belts with steel clips on them. They pulled them on over their jeans and buckled them securely at the waist.

Mark doubled the rope and coiled it again. "You guys can clip this rope to your belts," he told them. "I'll hold the rope on this side until you're across. Then you can hold it for me, and I'll come over."

They went out into the blizzard, which still showed no signs of letting up. Shane peered carefully through the falling snow for any sign of Grat. The old man's deep footprints, almost covered over already by the blowing snow, led to the trail that went back down the mountain.

Mark led them to the edge of the narrow ledge. It was only about two feet wide, with a flat rock face rising on one side, and a long sickening drop into nothing on the other. It was snowing so hard, Shane couldn't see how far the drop was. This was where Martin Grat had fallen to his death two centuries earlier.

"Here's the spike," Mark said, showing the steel stake someone had hammered into the side of the cliff, ten feet back from where the ledge began. He started tying the doubled-up rope to it.

"The ledge has totally crumbled away in the middle," Lynn said, eyeing the path they had to follow.

When Shane looked closer, he realized she was right. Halfway along the ten-foot distance, the rock had broken away, leaving a narrow V-shaped gap about a foot wide.

"You can step across that part," Mark assured them.

"Look on the positive side," Shane told Lynn, trying to make a joke. "At least there're no ghosts."

Shane and Lynn clipped their web belts to the safety rope. Shane went first, stepping carefully out onto the narrow ledge, and edging his way across it, inch by inch. The wind had blown most of the snow away, but the rock under his boots was still icy. A moment later, Lynn followed, pressing herself against the rock wall, her back to the blank drop.

When Shane was halfway across, he spotted the gap of missing rock and took a wide step. He flattened himself against the rock. Then he slid his left foot further along, and slowly, carefully, moved his right foot over.

When he was on the other side of the gap, he felt himself take a huge, ragged breath. He hadn't been aware of how scared he really was until after he'd done it. Lynn was edging her way along, and had almost reached the gap.

"Here, take my hand," Shane shouted to her. He reached out his arm, and his gloved fingers closed around

Lynn's. He gripped her hand tightly, and pulled as she stepped across. They were both over.

Shane glanced ahead. They only had about four feet to go until they reached the wider trail on the other side of the ledge. He felt the safety rope that held him and Lynn suddenly pulled taut so they couldn't move any further. He looked over at Mark. The other boy hadn't started following them yet.

"Give us some slack!" he shouted over the wind. "We can't move."

Instead of reacting, Mark stood on the other side of the ledge, staring at Shane and Lynn with a strange, insolent expression on his face. He pulled the safety rope tighter.

"We need some slack," Lynn shouted.

Mark stared back at them and laughed. He shucked his knapsack off his shoulder. It fell open at his feet. A red plaid jacket tumbled out and lay on the snow like a spot of blood.

Shane couldn't believe his eyes. "That's Grat's jacket!" he shouted.

"That's right!" Mark shouted back at them. "I stole it from old man Grat's house. Just to set you guys up!"

Shane felt a sinking realization, and suddenly, like finding the missing piece of a jigsaw puzzle, he realized the truth. "You! You're the one who sabotaged the Winter Murals! It wasn't Grat at all—it was you!"

"That's right!" Mark laughed. "And now get ready for the last Tug-of-War you'll ever play. Because I'm going to pull you right off the ledge!"

CHAPTER 17

"I've got you where I want you!" Mark shouted. "You thought you could just come along and take away the Quincy Cup from me. Now you're going to pay the price!"

Mark yanked hard on the rope. Shane and Lynn felt it tugging at their belts, pulling them toward the gap on the ledge.

"Don't, Mark!" Lynn shouted in a frightened voice. "We'll fall and be killed!"

Mark laughed cruelly. "Just like Martin Grat did two hundred years ago. And it'll all be an accident. A terrible, tragic accident. Except that I'll be Northwood's hero. Because after I get rid of you two, I'm going into Peace Lake to get medical help for everyone."

"You—!" Shane broke off, too astonished by his own realization. "*You* poisoned everyone!"

Mark laughed again. "It's amazing what a little rat poison will do. Of course, your friend Peter is such a pig,

112

he'll probably die. But everyone else will recover. And like I said, I'll be the hero for getting help."

Shane thought quickly. The gap was barely an inch away, and the rock ledge was treacherously icy. There was nothing to hold onto. If Mark started pulling again, it would be all over for him and Lynn. He had to keep Mark talking until he thought of something.

"You're the one who piled those rocks on the ski trail, aren't you?" Shane shouted at Mark. "And you cut the rope on our toboggan." While he spoke, he pressed his hand across the rock face in front of him, searching for a cranny or crevice that he could hold on to.

"Smart boy," Mark gloated. "Yeah, that's right. But first I snuck over to the Grat's the night before and stole his jacket and hat and his snowshoes. I'd been spying on him for weeks, and I knew he didn't lock his doors. So after he went to bed, I just went over and helped myself.

"Then I set up the rocks and cut the toboggan rope. And in case anyone spotted me, all they'd see was a red jacket and a red hat. They'd think it was a Grat attack. Just like they'll think it was Grat who somehow put the rat poison in the fudge sauce."

"Except there's no way Grat could get into Northwood's kitchen," Shane pointed out. "And you're a kitchen worker. They'll figure it out sooner or later, Mark. You'll never get away with it." Just then, Shane's fingers slipped into a narrow crack in the rock. It was just enough to give him a little bit of a hold.

The cruel smile left Mark's face. He stared through the swirling snowflakes at Shane and Lynn, his eyes filled with hatred, and his mouth frozen in a sneer. "Wrong, dudes," he yelled at them. "I will get away with it. And you'll be dead."

With those words, Mark yanked hard on the rope.

Shane felt himself pulled forward, his feet slipping on the ledge. He tightened his grip in the crevice, but he knew it couldn't hold him if Mark kept pulling. Beside him, Lynn screamed as her right foot slid into the gap. She began to teeter on the edge. Instantly, Shane reached out and grabbed her arm, pulling her back.

Then he felt the rope pulling again, harder and harder.

"We have to pull back!" Shane told Lynn. He dug his left hand deeper into the crack, and with his right hand gripped the rope. Lynn grabbed the rope, too, and together they started pulling against Mark's efforts. Once again, they were fighting a tug-of-war contest—but this time it was a fight to the death.

"You haven't got a chance!" Mark shouted, redoubling his efforts and pulling harder. Once again, Shane and Lynn felt the rope drawing them closer and closer to the edge of the ledge.

Suddenly, Shane saw a great dark shadow materialize through the blizzard behind Mark. A gust of wind blew aside the snowflakes for a moment. Shane recognized the huge, bearded figure of Cornelius Grat. The crazy old man stomped forward and picked up his coat from the snow where it had fallen.

"Now I have proof! You're the thief who stole my jacket!" Grat screamed, coming toward Mark.

114

Mark almost jumped a foot into the air. He dropped the rope and spun around.

"Help us!" Shane shouted, scarcely able to believe that he was asking Grat, of all people. "Help! He's trying to kill us!"

Grat looked over and spotted the two kids on the ledge. His mouth fell open in amazement. He looked from Mark to Shane and Lynn, taking in the rope and the spike nailed into the cliff.

"I'll save you!" Grat shouted at them. "Don't move. I'll—"

Suddenly Mark charged at the old man and butted him hard in the middle. Grat staggered, his arms flailing in the air as he tried to regain his balance. Mark swung with his fist and connected again.

Grat screamed and fell backward. He disappeared over the edge of the plateau. His wail of terror as he fell was rapidly drowned out by the rising howl of the vicious wind.

Meanwhile, Shane's hand had been fumbling at the knot holding his web belt to the rope. His gloves made it impossible to untie. He was about to pull them off his hands, when Mark ran back to the rope and pulled it tight again.

It was Tug-of-War all over again, and once again, Shane and Lynn felt themselves being pulled closer and closer to the edge.

This is it, Shane thought. *There's no way out*.

"Mark, please!" Lynn sobbed. "Please don't do this to us."

115

Once again, the wind blew them Mark's cruel laughter in reply.

Then, through the snowflakes swirling around Mark, Shane saw a strange glow, as if someone was shining a greenish-yellow light on the side of Mount Fear. A figure strode into view behind Mark.

It was a tall man, dressed in an old-fashioned buckskin coat and pants, with fringed leggings tied up around his knees. The man moved smoothly and serenely along the plateau toward Mark, almost as if he were floating on the surface of the snow. The greenish-yellow light formed an aura around him. His skin was deathly white and his long, bushy sideburns and cleft chin made him instantly recognizable to Shane. It was the face from the old portrait in the dining hall—the face of a man who'd been dead for two hundred years.

It was the ghost of Benjamin Quincy!

Sensing that Shane and Lynn were looking at something behind him, Mark glanced over his shoulder and saw the spectral figure. The ghost looked at Mark. Slowly, Benjamin Quincy's arms rose, and he reached toward him.

There was a moment when only the wind howled. Then Mark screamed with utter terror.

The ghost began to move toward him.

"No!" Mark screamed. "No, get back."

Still, the figure moved closer. Mark dropped the rope, and backed away, but there were only two ways to go— onto the narrow ledge where Shane and Lynn stood frozen in terror or over the edge of the cliff.

"No! You're not real! Stop it!" Mark screamed in panic. He took another step back, but this time his foot met air. He staggered slightly, turning his eyes to Shane and Lynn. "Help—"

And then Mark plunged over the edge, a last terrible scream fading behind him as he fell.

Shane and Lynn didn't dare move. They looked across the narrow ledge, where the ghost stood, silent and still. The supernatural creature turned his burning eyes on them. Shane felt a shiver of terror ripple up his spine. Now it's our turn, he thought, certain they would meet the same fate as Mark at the hands of the ghost.

Then, as they watched, the ghost moved forward, and loosed the rope from the piton. The eerie glow around the specter began to fade. Shane saw a strange expression appear on Benjamin Quincy's ghostly face—a look almost of happiness, or relief.

The ghost raised an arm, as if it were saluting the two students. It threw down the rope, giving Shane and Lynn enough slack to get off the ledge. Then, the ghost disappeared into thin air—like a lightbulb blinking out.

Shane heaved a sigh of relief. He reached out and squeezed Lynn's hand.

"Did you see that?" Lynn asked in an awed whisper.

"Yeah, I saw it," Shane told her.

"What should we do now?"

"The ghost is gone—and so is Mark. But Northwood still needs a doctor," Shane pointed out. "Let's keep going."

CHAPTER 18

Shane looked out the dining hall window at the thin pink line of dawn forming on the eastern horizon. Outside, the lights of emergency vehicles—ambulances, state trooper cars, and even a snowplow—blinked silently in the early morning light. The jagged peak of Mount Fear was bathed in crimson from the rising sun.

The blizzard was over, and winds were pushing the clouds away to the south, leaving behind clear sky. Lights bobbed on the side of Mount Fear—not ghost lights along the treacherous ledge that led to Peace Lake, but the lights of search-and-rescue teams, looking for signs of Mark Lepine and Cornelius Grat in the dark forests along the terrible mountain's lower slopes.

"A new day," Lynn said quietly. She was sitting beside Shane on a bench near the door. They were still bundled up in their warm winter clothing, because the dining hall's double doors were wide open. Paramedics in white jackets carried a student on a stretcher toward the waiting doors of an ambulance outside.

Shane nodded silently. "And a new beginning. I mean, after last night—"

"I know," Lynn interrupted. "It was so scary. I want to put it behind us for good."

After Mark's fall, and their strange rescue by the glowing apparition on Mount Fear, Shane and Lynn had struggled on to get help for Northwood. Once on the other side of the narrow ledge, they had trekked downhill for another hour before finally staggering into Peace Lake in the early hours of the morning, exhausted and cold.

When they told their story to the state troopers, the sheriff immediately ordered out a snowplow to clear the road to Northwood. A long line of police cars and ambulances followed, carrying doctors, nurses, and several dozen volunteers who made up a search-and-rescue team.

Ambulances had taken Peter and the sickest students back to the hospital in Peace Lake. The rest of the students and teachers still had fevers and stomachaches. But they were alive and, according to the doctors, getting better.

Shane looked up and noticed the lights of the search-and-rescue crews on the slopes of Mount Fear moving downhill. He pointed them out to Lynn.

"Maybe they've found them," Lynn said.

"I hope so. I hope they're still alive," Shane added.

Lynn was quiet a moment. Then she said, "I hope Grat is alive because he tried to rescue us. But Mark . . ."

"Mark had a sick mind," Shane pointed out. "If he's alive, maybe doctors can help him."

The Quince walked slowly up the steps with a state

trooper beside him. He still looked sick, but when he saw Shane and Lynn, his eyes lit up.

"You're both heroes," he said, sliding carefully onto the bench beside them.

"Are you feeling okay?" Lynn asked, looking at the headmaster with concern.

"Much better!" the Quince said, even mustering a little enthusiasm. "The doctor gave me some medicine and it's already beginning to work. I simply don't know what to say about Mark." He shook his head sadly.

"Mark was setting everyone up so he could win the Winter Murals," Shane said. "He sabotaged the races and tried to make it look like Grat was doing it."

"And when he lost he tried to kill everyone and get credit as a hero," Lynn finished.

"According to what you've told us, Mark tried to pull you both off the ledge, but fell off himself instead," the state trooper said. "Is there anything else you'd like to add?"

Shane and Lynn exchanged a look. They both knew that they had kept part of the story—the part about the ghost of Benjamin Quincy—to themselves.

"No," Lynn said, looking up at the state trooper. She looked at Shane.

Shane shook his head. "No," he repeated. "I can't think of anything we left out."

"I do have some good news," the Quince said, a slight smile spreading across his face. "Peter and the other students who were taken to the hospital are going to be fine!"

Just then, Shane saw one of the searchers running up the steps of the dining hall. The man stomped his boots, and brushed snow off the bright orange vest he wore over his ski coat.

"We found Cornelius Grat!" he shouted to the state trooper.

The headmaster rose suddenly, his face filled with apprehension. "Is he . . . ?"

The man nodded. "He's a very lucky man. Some deep snowdrifts cushioned his fall. His legs are broken, and he's had some frostbite. But he's alive."

"Mark?" Shane asked. He was afraid to hear the answer.

The man looked at Shane and Lynn and shook his head. "We found him too, but he didn't make it. He hit some rocks. He was killed instantly."

A heavy silence fell over the gathering.

The Quince gazed past the doors of the dining hall, and Shane followed his eyes. The rescue teams, in their bright orange vests, were emerging from the forest. They carried two stretchers. One was completely covered. On the other was the enormous bulk of Northwood's eccentric neighbor.

"From now on, the Quincy and the Grats will be friends, not enemies," the Quince vowed. He looked at Shane and Lynn. "I know he's a scary old man, but believe it or not, when we were boys growing up in this valley, we were friends. Cornelius has a heart of gold, but he hides it behind all his anger."

"He must have some good in him," Shane agreed.

"Because when he saw what Mark was doing on the ledge, he tried to rescue us."

"It's so sad," said Lynn. "I mean, the way he lives all alone in that house that's falling down."

The Quince's eyes lit up. "I know what I'll do. Northwood will adopt Cornelius's old house as a school fix-up project. Just like we built the new barn last year." Mr. Quincy looked suddenly very pleased. "I'm going out to make that offer right now."

With that, the Quince marched down the steps, leaving Shane and Lynn alone. Shane glanced over at the oil painting of the headmaster's ancestor. The dour face of Benjamin Quincy in the Continental Army uniform stared sternly down at them.

"I guess we're the only ones who'll ever know the real story of what happened on Mount Fear last night," Lynn said. "I mean, no one else would believe us if we told them a ghost rescued us from Mark. They'd think we imagined it because we had such a terrible experience."

Shane nodded slowly. "Except Peter. I didn't believe him when he said he saw a ghost on Mount Fear last Halloween. And everyone else just teased him about it. When he's out of the hospital, we'll have to tell him everything. We owe it to him."

"And it was the ghost of Benjamin Quincy, not Martin Grat, just like Peter said," Lynn said. "Do you think Ben Quincy pushed Martin Grat off the mountain two hundred years ago so he could buy up the Grat land?"

"I guess so," Shane answered slowly. "That must be why his ghost appeared, instead of Martin Grat's. Like

Peter said, Ben Quincy was doomed to haunt Mount Fear until he paid for his crime.''

As Shane spoke, he remembered his last image of the spectral figure, the strange look of relief on Ben Quincy's glowing face, and the arm raised in a farewell salute.

''Maybe by rescuing us he made up for the murder, so now he can go to his rest,'' Shane concluded.

''We'll never know for sure,'' Lynn sighed. ''But I have a feeling about one thing.''

''What's that?''

Lynn smiled, certain she was right. ''I bet the ghost lights people saw on Mount Fear are gone forever.''